Photographing in the Cleveland Flats, about 1928.

FOR THE WORLD TO SEE

THE LIFE OF

Margaret Bourke-White

COMPILED, EDITED AND

WITH A BIOGRAPHICAL NARRATIVE BY

JONATHAN SILVERMAN

———

PREFACE BY

ALFRED EISENSTAEDT

———

A STUDIO BOOK · THE VIKING PRESS · *NEW YORK*

For my mother, my sister Amy, my grandmother Bella, my aunt Renée

—

Previously unpublished Margaret Bourke-White photographs and writings, and the compilation and editing throughout, copyright © 1983 by Roger White, Executor of the Estate of Margaret Bourke-White.

Biographical narrative copyright © 1983 by Jonathan Silverman.

For Margaret Bourke-White's previously published writings included in extracts and quotations, copyright Margaret Bourke-White and renewed by her and/or by her Estate as follows:

"DEAR FATHERLAND, REST QUIETLY" copyright 1946, renewed © 1974
EYES ON RUSSIA copyright 1931, renewed © 1959
HALFWAY TO FREEDOM copyright 1949, renewed © 1977
PORTRAIT OF MYSELF © 1963
PURPLE HEART VALLEY copyright 1944, renewed © 1972
SHOOTING THE RUSSIAN WAR copyright 1942, renewed © 1970

Grateful acknowledgment is made to Syracuse University and to the Estate of Margaret Bourke-White for the use of materials in the George Arents Research Library for Special Collections at Syracuse University.

Acknowledgment is made for permission to reproduce additional copyrighted materials as follows: the letter from Edward Weston on page 78, © 1981 Arizona Board of Regents, Center for Creative Photography; quotations on pages 74 and 77 from articles by Margaret Bourke-White, copyright 1935 by *Nation* magazine, The Nation Associates, Inc.; quotations on page 190 from Irving Penn's speech at the Museum of Modern Art Symposium on November 20, 1950.

LIBRARY OF CONGRESS CATALOGING IN PUBLICATION DATA

Silverman, Jonathan.
  For the world to see.
  (A Studio book)
Bibliography: p. 216
  Includes index.
  1. Bourke-White, Margaret, 1904–1971.
2. Photographers—United States—Biography.
I. Bourke-White, Margaret, 1904–1971. II. Title.
TR140.B6S59 1983   770′.92′4 [B]   82-17348
ISBN 0-670-32356-X

Grateful acknowledgment is made to the following people and organizations for permission to reproduce photographs as follows:

Estate of Margaret Bourke-White: photographs on pages 40 and 42 copyright 1931, renewed © 1959; pages 127 and 130 copyright 1939 by Erskine Caldwell and Margaret Bourke-White, renewed © 1967 by Erskine Caldwell; pages 16, 17, 43, 48, 55 © 1972, and seventy-six additional previously unpublished photographs throughout copyright © 1983 by Roger White, Executor of the Estate of Margaret Bourke-White.

Time Incorporated: photographs taken on assignment for *Life* magazine as follows: page 125, copyright 1936, renewed © 1964; page 124, copyright 1937, renewed © 1965; pages 107, 134 copyright 1941, renewed © 1969; pages 112–13, 138–39, copyright 1943, renewed © 1971; pages 109, 136–37, 145 copyright 1944, renewed © 1972; pages 158, 162 copyright 1945, renewed © 1973; pages 159, 164–65, 177, 179 copyright 1946, renewed © 1974; page 180, copyright 1947, renewed © 1975; pages 184–85, copyright 1949, renewed © 1977; pages 198–99, copyright 1950, renewed © 1978; page 213, copyright 1951, renewed © 1979; pages 207, 209 copyright 1952, renewed © 1980; page 212, copyright 1954, renewed © 1982; page 191 © 1959; page 166 © 1960; previously unpublished photographs on pages 122–23, 132–33, 135, 140–44, 146–49, 156–57, 160–61, 163, 167, 178, 181–83, 196–97, 200–206, 208, 210–11 copyright © 1983 by Time Incorporated.

Berenice Abbott: photograph on page 9.

The British Broadcasting Corporation: photograph on page 104.

Magnum: photograph on page 173 by Bob Henriques, © 1961 Magnum.

Printed in the United States of America

CONTENTS

ACKNOWLEDGMENTS

The completion of this book depended on the trust, assistance, and encouragement of many people. It would be impossible, in so short a space, to list them all. But there are several whose names I can't, in good conscience, omit. They are: Roger B. White, Roger White, Jr., and Jonathan White, the executor and the legatees of the Estate of Margaret Bourke-White; Scott Meredith and Sidney Meredith, the best literary agents in the business; Jack Scovil, who was particularly helpful; Olga Zaferatos, my patient and caring editor; Sidney Huttner, Head of the George Arents Research Library, Syracuse University; Ralph Graves, Mary Jane McGonegal and Beth Zarcone of Time, Inc.; Gael Towey Dillon, the book's designer; Howard C. Daitz, Bourke-White collector; my friends Samuel A. Abady, Wayne Forsythe, Andy Rabin, Jeff Kocher and Peri Petras, Dr. Jeff Marqusee, John and Janet Marqusee; and my constant companion—Karen Haight.

Margaret Bourke-White and I met in 1936. We were going to be colleagues—fellow *Life* photographers—but I knew right away that we were also going to be friends.

The early years at *Life* were very hectic, so much so that we, as well as Peter Stackpole, Tom McAvoy, and, later, Carl Mydans—the other staff photographers—had as many assignments as we could manage each day. Consequently, we didn't see much of each other, and most of the time we didn't even know what the others were shooting. Frequently we were working at opposite ends of the world. During the later part of Margaret Bourke-White's life, when Parkinson's disease kept her closer to home, I saw more of her. My late wife and I were often invited for weekend lunches at her home in Connecticut. I remember well those afternoons of wonderful meals and conversation. Maggie was a splendid hostess and a delightful raconteuse.

People have said to me that I am the photographer's photographer. I think that Margaret Bourke-White was more that than I. People were in awe of her. Her name was magical. She was a star during a great era in photography, and *Life* was proud to claim her as one of its own. Maggie was vivacious, articulate, and very charming. She was also enormously attractive. But most of all, she was fully dedicated to her work. She was married to her cameras. No assignment was too small for her. If she had been asked to photograph a bread crumb at five-thirty in the morning, she would have arrived for the session at five. She had a great inner drive and a passion for whatever she did. At that time, forty years ago, she was singular in being a woman photographer who had the courage and drive to go after the action, even if that meant that she would find herself in dangerous surroundings. If she were alive today, Maggie would be in the forefront of the women's movement. Being female did not discourage her from doing exactly what she wanted to do. And what she did, she did brilliantly.

Like all of us at *Life,* she pursued what she did for the glory of *Life* and for the glory of her country. We were no-nonsense people, part of an élite group, pioneers of photojournalism in America. Maggie's contributions to photojournalism are considerable. But her dedication and determination to show the world as it is are the qualities by which I remember her most and because of which I can truly say that Margaret Bourke-White was a remarkable person.

Alfred Eisenstaedt
New York City
July 1982

"I understand that you want some kind of a biographical sketch. At the age of twenty-five it is hard to write anything that can be called by such a dignified name as a biographical sketch, but I shall give you a few facts."

That was how Margaret Bourke-White prefaced the story of her life in the resumé she kept on file for the press and other interested parties in 1930, when her illustrious career was just beginning. Some thirty years later, when her autobiography, *Portrait of Myself*, appeared, Bourke-White was hailed by her publishers as "the first photographer to see the artistic and storytelling possibilities in American industry, the first to write social criticism with a lens, and the most distinguished and venturesome foreign correspondent with a camera to report wars, politics and social and political revolution on three continents." In 1963, the year *Portrait of Myself* came out, those were a few of the facts. The complete facts of Bourke-White's career make an epic adventure.

She was attracted to heights, adored flying, and before her death in 1971 she had flown in every manner of airship, from the primitive Curtiss Robin to an early supersonic jet fighter, photographing the earth from airplanes and also the airplanes themselves.

Although she was devoted foremost to photography—"It is my trade—and my deep joy"—she also had a talent for and a love of writing: she wrote five books of her own, plus her autobiography, and four other book projects on which she collaborated with others.

Bourke-White defied the prevalent stereotype of womanhood in many ways. It was considered rebellious for a woman to dare to compete in business on the same terms as a man, but Bourke-White had no qualms about doing that. She competed on the basis of merit, the common denominator of all professionals. Furthermore, she had to work harder than most men and get better results because she knew that "in the beginning people don't take a woman so seriously and are afraid to trust her on a job. Or they think she is going to get married in the next ten minutes and won't finish it. Or they think that she is too temperamental to work with."

Many of her feats would seem less exceptional if she had been a man. In fact, her earliest coup (taking dramatic photographs of the story of steelmaking) was surely not sufficiently historic to make news. But because she was a woman, and an extremely attractive one at that, she interested the press.

She was such a tremendous magnet for publicity that rumors spread that Bourke-White was just a front, that there was some male photographer taking the pictures, and that she had some kind of clever publicity agent or businessman who made her look as though she was the operator. But aside from that and the conventional prejudices, Bourke-White felt a woman had one great advantage that outweighed the disadvantages: "people are much more willing to help her if she shows any signs of getting along at all."

From 1928 until 1936 Bourke-White's livelihood depended, for the most part, on her photographing the practices and products of a wide variety of industries: pigs, watches, oil, salt, natural gas, automobiles, fish, sweat shops, paper mills, power, and skyscrapers, to name a few. But she began her industrial period photographing steel mills, the most basic of manufacturing industries, and the industry she obviously liked best. "There is something dynamic about the rush of flowing metal, the dying sparks, the clouds of smoke, the heat, the traveling cranes clanging back and forth," she said. That dynamic "something" in the making of steel is what Bourke-White set out to capture on film in the winter of 1928, when she got her first steel-mill job at the Otis Steel Mill in Cleveland, Ohio.

Steel had not been photographed before with a view toward the drama and visual excitement of the subject, and the work was infinitely harder than Bourke-White had imagined; but because she was very eager to record the live power she saw in the maw of the great Otis blast furnace, she persevered.

» The first few weeks all my negatives went into the waste basket . . . so many things went wrong. I would get a little burst of yellow smoke in the lens and all the work went for nothing. Sometimes the traveling cranes would tremble and everything would be blurred. Sometimes it was so hot that the varnish on my camera would rise up in blisters and I had a coat of tan as though I had been to Florida. At times I kept a line of men lined behind me bucket brigade fashion and as often as I made exposures I handed the holders back to get the films out of the heat. Finally I had a collection of twelve pictures. Literally hundreds of films had been thrown away. . . . In no other photographic situation that I can think of will one find the technical difficulties that exist in steel mills but I learned a great deal that was valuable for me to learn. «

Not least of all, she learned there was money to be made photographing the story of steel. The president of Otis Steel was so impressed with her "pioneering work" that he agreed to pay her $100 per picture—ten times her usual fee. The twelve photos were reprinted in a promotional booklet for the Otis stockholders, a publication that quickly became the envy of other manufacturing companies, such as Republic Steel and Chrysler Inc. who then commissioned Bourke-White to make photographs of their plants.

Photographing steel became a good little business for Bourke-White, but it was also an artistic endeavor. In the making of steel Bourke-White found a subject that had tremendous visual power as well as an evocative power that came from the larger subject of steel's role in the life of the world at that time. The late 1920s were the apex of the Industrial Age and to Bourke-White's eyes "at the very heart of industry, with the most drama, the most beauty" was steel. Steel was the industry that launched her career. Nevertheless, there was obviously a limit to the number of steel-mill pictures she could take before she began repeating herself. She knew that it was "disastrous to stick to a technique or formula of which the public approves simply because the public will buy it."

"This is a big wonderful world," she said, "and people, especially artists, should grow in it, because artists show others the world." The dangers involved in taking photographs of industry were of little consequence to Bourke-White. "I suppose I have been in a few tight places," she was quoted as saying in 1929. "Cinder and ore piles will slide away beneath one. I was buried up to my neck in iron dust once, trying to get the view I wanted of some smokestacks seen from there. But they pulled me out and I've learned how to pick firmer footholds, I guess." The fact is, she often went to risky extremes for the sake of a single photograph. Bourke-White's personal code hinged on her being able to produce a picture under any set of conditions. Furthermore, although industry was dangerous, Bourke-White was so impassioned with the creative potential she perceived in industrial subjects, so eager to record her perceptions, that she let nothing stand in her way. The keen enthusiasm

Margaret Bourke-White, age 25. Photograph by Berenice Abbott.

she brought to her work overflows at one point in her 1930 resumé: "Art that springs from industry should have real flesh and blood because industry is the vital force of this great age."

Among photographers of industry Bourke-White is unique in expressing such feelings. The idea that her photographs not only recorded the beauty of her subjects, but also interpreted the age in which she lived, and conveyed its spirit, is the germ of a larger conception about photography as an art which Bourke-White originated. Edward Weston, for example, photographed Armco Steel in Akron, Ohio, in the early 1920s, and according to Weston's biographer, Ben Maddow, the sharp focus and attention to volumetric form that distinguish Weston's unique style were qualities that first appeared in those steel-mill photographs Weston did in Akron. But there is no indication that Weston ever wanted to convey an impression of history in his Armco pictures.

Atop the Terminal Tower, Cleveland, 1929.

Alfred Stieglitz, Alvin Langdon Coburn, Charles Sheeler, and Paul Strand photographed industrial subjects too, but their aim was not to interpret history. In the great tradition of photography as a fine art, photographs of industrial subjects by those photographers abstract beautiful forms and patterns in the manner of paintings and sculpture, a technique that formed a basis for defending photography as a fine art.

Although Bourke-White had contact with Stieglitz, Weston, and Strand in the 1930s, her aesthetic principles had really nothing to do with those of the masters. She frankly admitted in 1929 interview that she didn't know the traditions of photography. "I've had to work out my own technique," she said. "I know when I get the picture I want . . . even if I can't quite explain the process." But typically, she could explain her purpose. "Art can never stand off with skirts spread away from the touch of things in the raw, in the making," she said. "The purpose of art is to find beauty in the big thing of the age. Today that big thing is industry."

The idea that the big thing of the age was industry and that there was an allure in it that could be communicated dramatically in a graphic medium had occurred also to Henry Luce, who launched *Fortune* in 1930 as a magazine that would tell industry's story. Luce had been publishing *Time* for seven years by 1930, but the only serious use *Time* made of pictures then was on the front cover, where a portrait of the week's most important personage would appear. Luce saw, however, that photographs would have to play a large part in fulfilling *Fortune*'s purpose, which in his view was to convey "the dignity, and the beauty, the smartness and excitement of modern industry"; and that's where Margaret Bourke-White came in.

On May 8, 1929, Henry Luce sent the following wire to Bourke-White: "Harold Wengler has shown me your photographs. Would like to see you. Could you come to New York within a week at our expense. Please telegraph when." The wire was signed Henry Luce, Time Inc. Since Bourke-White had no interest in photographing politicians, she did not understand why the publisher of *Time* magazine would ask to see her. But she was curious. Even if nothing came of meeting with Luce she felt she could use the trip to New York to solicit business at advertising agencies in the city; and besides, Luce was picking up the tab. So Bourke-White wired back on May 9, confirming her willingness to come.

Her Otis Steel photographs were the ones that had captivated Henry Luce. Although Harold Wengler had shown the pictures to Luce personally, within that very fortnight Bourke-White's Otis pictures had also run in the rotogravure sections of several Midwestern newspapers, and less than a week before Luce had wired her the *New York Sun* published a feature about Bourke-White that carried the eye-catching title, "Dizzy Heights Have No Terror for This Girl Photographer, Who Braves Numerous Perils to Film the Beauty of Iron and Steel."

Steel was Bourke-White's forte but she had already begun to diversify, entering into every possible industry to do the kind of promotional photographs needed by the advertising departments of large manufacturing corporations. Another feature article about her, "Girl Photographer," published by the NEA syndicate in 1929, reported that a giant electric corporation, which also manufactured streetcars, had commissioned her to take the most effective picture she could of a city's congestion at home-going time. The picture had to be beautiful but, above all, tell the story of the need for more streetcars. For weeks Bourke-White canvassed the buildings adjacent to Cleveland's Terminal Tower, where her studio was located for most of 1929 and 1930, asking for the privilege of seeing what she could see out of certain windows, and finally she found a piece of iron grillwork that made a perfect frame for a befitting scene (of crowds of commuters below waiting for streetcars).

Bourke-White's main source for industrial-promotion assignments before she relocated to New York in November 1930 was the Meldrum and Fewsmith Agency in Cleveland. Joe Fewsmith was her main contact there. He was the one who secured her commissions to photograph Republic Steel and Chrysler, both of which were Meldrum and Fewsmith advertising clients. Fewsmith taught her the basics of advertising work and also helped pave the way for her when she moved to New York by writing to his friends at ad agencies there.

Fortune endowed Bourke-White's photography with national exposure and gave her a chance to cover a wider variety of industries and to travel more extensively than she had ever dreamed possible. But even before she worked for *Fortune* Bourke-White had won considerable prominence on her own. In fact, the appearance of Bourke-White's steel photographs in the final dummy of the first issue of *Fortune* was the deciding factor for dozens of advertisers who, on the basis of the magazine's impressive illustrations, agreed to gamble on buying space in it.

Less than a month after meeting with Bourke-White and borrowing her steel photographs, Luce had sold enough ad pages to fill several *Fortune* issues. Bourke-White then received a letter from Parker Lloyd-Smith, the magazine's managing editor: "This is to inform you officially of what you might conceivably have suspected. That we are glad to accept your proposition of giving us half your time from July 1. The cash consideration being $1000 a month."

Bourke-White reserved half her time for private commissions, such as those that came from Meldrum and Fewsmith, because she could not afford to tie herself exclusively to the magazine. Her personal gross income in 1929 was over $20,000. Although *Fortune* would obviously bring her additional riches, she primarily saw the magazine as an opportunity to do the sort of work that most interested her, and as a vehicle that would bring her photography and her

Commuters waiting for streetcars, Cleveland, 1929.

name to a wide audience. So it is small wonder she wrote the following to her mother upon receiving Lloyd-Smith's letter: "I feel as if the world has been opened up and I hold all the keys." The prospect of giving birth to a new magazine was exhilarating.

Bourke-White was *Fortune*'s only photographer for the eight months prior to the publication of the first issue in February 1930. From shoemaking at Lynn, Massachusetts, to commercial orchid raising in New Jersey, to meat-packing at the Chicago stockyards, there was no location or type of photography too difficult or too mundane for her.

She worked with Archibald MacLeish on a story about the Elgin Watch factory, where they were both enchanted by the exquisite shapes of minute watch parts. She also worked with young Dwight Macdonald (who was fresh out of college and according to Henry Luce "a rough diamond") on the Corning Glass factory electric light bulb plant. They were fortunate on that assignment to find an artisan of a vanishing craft, "a giant of a glassblower who stood high on a pedestal and with

At the Artists' Ball in Greenwich Village, 1934, wearing a costume made of her industrial photographs.

the power of his lungs and skill of his lips, blew golden-hot nuggets into huge bulbs, streetlight size. The making of all other types of light bulbs was mechanized, and within weeks of our visit, these last handmade, or mouth made streetlamps yielded to mechanization also."

Henry Luce himself went out with Bourke-White on one assignment: a series of articles published in *Fortune* under the title "The Unseen Half of South Bend." Luce wanted to portray a world he felt many Americans had never been shown, the behind-the-scenes integration of the working life of an entire industrial city—South Bend, Indiana. Luce and Bourke-White covered the manufacture of plow blades, automobiles, brakes, varnish, sewing machines, toys, and fishing tackle. The approach Luce took taught Bourke-White a great deal. Whereas she would aim to make the most striking compositions, she found while working with Luce that searching for "the integrated whole required a much wider

conception. It added another dimension to photography. It gave the camera one more task: pictures could be beautiful, but must tell facts too." And the idea of searching for the "unseen half" was, Bourke-White decided, an invaluable habit for a photographer to form for use in many places besides South Bend.

Her *Fortune* assignments also gave her opportunities to expand her reputation for being able to take photographs under the most extreme physical conditions. One episode she frequently recounted was how she went about photographing a lumber camp on the Gatineau River in Canada for a story on the International Paper Company. "I ran into lots of difficulties on this particular job," she said in a 1933 lecture. "I was taking pictures at 37 degrees below zero. I wouldn't have minded that so much but I had a lot of trouble with the camera. It was very difficult to set it up on the snow. I would just get it set and one leg of the tripod would go sliding off. When I tried to take the pictures, I found my shutter was frozen so that sometimes the shutter would click and sometimes it wouldn't." She couldn't believe that any photographs would come out, with all the equipment failure she experienced, but indeed they did and she jokingly concluded that a camera wasn't needed to take pictures. "All you have to do," she said, "is clap your hands and you have a picture."

Another extreme situation in which she prevailed was in a Pennsylvania coal mine.

» I spent a month there doing a study of the anthracite field for the *Fortune* people and every day I put a light on my cap like a miner and went one thousand feet below the earth to take photographs. Miners are very superstitious. In some mines they will throw down their picks and go home for the day if a woman so much as enters the mines. Anything out of the way makes them jittery. But I had persuaded them to let me go ahead with my work and they were beginning to get more or less used to seeing me around. One day I wanted to get a certain kind of pitch mining that was going on underground four miles away from the shaft. We started out and everything went wrong. We took one of the little automatic mules and that got out of order. We started walking and our way was constantly being blocked because we were a little fidgety but at last we got to a place where the pitch mining was going on. We crawled up a little slope into the pitch pocket. . . the fire boss going ahead to test for gas. I got my camera set up, my lights in place, the electricians were busy insulating the wires for miles back so that we would not be blown up when we turned on the juice, I had drills placed in the walls and posed two miners. I called out to the man, "I am ready . . . throw on the lights." They turned on the lights, there was a bright flash of light and then darkness. They had thrown on too much power and had blown out my bulbs. I had more bulbs but they were four miles away—one thousand feet above the earth in my hotel. So there was nothing to do but pack up our stuff and start back. On the way back everything went wrong. We had to go along unused passages because our way was constantly blocked. We could hear water rushing in underground channels close to where we were. The miners were getting more and more nervous and finally one of them said, "You will have to do something about this, these men are getting nervous. What can you do, can you sing?" I do not sing for the public but I was willing to do anything then and we marched back through those four miles underground with me singing at the top of my voice. . . . At last we came to the foot of the shaft and when we got up above ground it was dark. I collected my light bulbs and went back the next day and then we got the picture. «

———

One of the great ironies in Bourke-White's career is that she was inside the First National Bank of Boston, photographing the bank's lobby and vault for advertisements that would appear in *Fortune*, on October 29, 1929, the night the stock market crashed. At that moment, Bourke-White was too busy trying to keep the bank's worried vice-presidents out of her camera's field of view to be concerned about the disaster that had just befallen the financial world. But much later she realized, in recalling the incident, that she was probably the only photographer inside a bank on that fateful night. She felt that if she had only had the presence of mind to photograph the worried bank officers frantically running around the bank she would have had an historic record. All she achieved, in this case, was to convey an impression of the First National that would instill confidence and faith in those who saw her photographs in the bank's advertisements.

During her industrial period Bourke-White adhered to some extent to the demands established for her as a commercial artist, but she also followed her

Margaret Bourke-White with coal miners in Pennsylvania, 1933.

own artistic nature. We traditionally think of true artists as people such as Weston and Stieglitz, who eschewed commercialism because they believed commercial attitudes and practices annihilated aesthetic experience. Bourke-White understood the difference between commercial art and true art, but for her there was no conflict between the two because she believed that art had to find beauty in the burning issue of the day, and in her day that issue was commerce: the products, practices, and activities of industry that made the Industrial Age what it was.

Bourke-White also saw an inherent beauty in industrial objects themselves, to which she was no doubt responding in her passion for machine forms. American philosopher John Dewey acknowledged the emergence of beauty in industry in his *Art as Experience*, in which he says: "There is something clean in the esthetic sense about a piece of machinery that has a logical structure that fits it for its work, and the polish of steel and copper that is essential to good performance is intrinsically pleasing in perception. If one compares the commercial products of the present with those of even twenty years ago, one is struck by the great gain in form and color. The change from the old wooden Pullman cars with their silly encumbering ornamentation to the steel cars of the present is typical of what I mean."

Dewey was writing, of course, in the early 1930s, and his statement closely echoes Bourke-White's own feelings about the beauty of machines: "It is only recently that artists have come to realize that a dynamo is as beautiful as a vase," she said. "It is

First National Bank, Boston, 1929.

beautiful because of the simplicity of its form." Bourke-White goes far beyond Dewey, however, in praising the beauty of machines. "Not only is the finished dynamo beautiful, but a dynamo under construction has artistic material and not only is the dynamo under construction beautiful, but the men who build that dynamo have a certain beauty—their faces have an artistic value because of the virility and importance of the work they do."

Bourke-White's photographs of industry clearly have more to do with the dramatic power of steel than with the "virility and importance" of workers' faces. It was a machine age she was working in, not an age of labor. Between 1919 and 1929, fewer and fewer people cared about the worker because business was booming, and thanks to business the average man and woman had a greater abundance of new goods to buy than ever before: electrical goods, such as the radio, refrigerator, and vacuum cleaner as well as heavier items, such as the automobile. In that machine environment Bourke-White saw the camera as a device that had suddenly come into its own as the most fitting medium of expression.

"There is some peculiar reason why the camera is so suitable for the portrayal of this age," she said in a 1933 lecture. "I think the very directness of photography has something to do with it. It is very clean-cut and direct and a very honest medium and I think perhaps the fact that the camera is a mechanical medium—that is, mechanical in its operation—has something to do with photography's being in such harmony with this age."

In content and form, therefore, the aim of Bourke-White's photography was to convey the dramatic power of the Industrial Age. Her photographs were recognized as art, frequently being exhibited in museums and winning prizes in annual salons. But beyond the sentiment of *objet d'art*, a sentiment that generally accompanies a work at a museum exhibition, Bourke-White's work achieved greater resonance and power precisely because her photographs also functioned as advertising and promotion for business and industry. Bourke-White's role in that chemistry that caused our consumer society to explode in the 1920s is illustrated by an anecdote told by the moderator of a 1934 conference on "Choosing a Career" when he introduced Bourke-White's talk: "I know from my own days in advertising agencies that when we had a difficult problem, if we had let us say a brand of peanuts that weren't selling very well at ten cents a bag because people didn't think they were worth ten cents, thought they were only five cent peanuts, usually the inevitable conference would be called, and after a half hour or so of collaboration, the conclusion of the conference would always be the same, the best thing to do would be to hire Miss Margaret Bourke-White to take a picture of the peanuts and then people would think they were worth twenty-five cents a bag."

International Harvester, 1933.

Open-hearth mill, Ford Motor Company, Detroit, 1929.

Republic Steel, 1929.

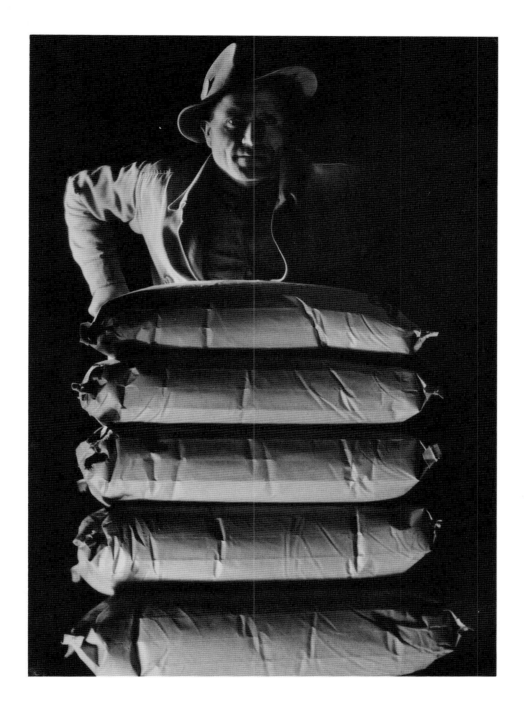

Laborer, Lehigh Portland Cement Co., 1930.

Aluminum Company of America, 1930.

Chrysler Corporation, 1929.

Erie Railroad, about 1931.

Mine passage, Hudson Coal, 1931.

Limestone quarry, Indiana, 1931.

George Washington Bridge under construction, about 1931.

Empire State Building, about 1931.

Street scene, New York City, about 1931.

Detail of a La Salle, about 1933.

The age of prosperity, of course, was as illusory as the twenty-five-cent bag of peanuts. Reversing a ten-year trend, American industrial production nosedived between 1929 and 1933, and new burning issues took the place of industrial vitality in America. One of the issues that emerged was the curious development of industrial vigor in the Soviet Union. In fact, while the industrial production of the United States fell by nearly half during those years, the industrial production of the Soviet Union nearly doubled. In 1928 Joseph Stalin had instituted the first Five-Year Plan, and in the wake of the great changes widely rumored to be occurring a great deal of speculation ensued as to what was actually happening under the new regime. Although a few determined foreign journalists had succeeded in getting stories out, no foreigner had been permitted to take photographs inside the Soviet Union since the 1917 revolution. No photographs of significance emerged from the Communist state until September 1930, when Margaret Bourke-White sailed back from Russia with 800 of her own, taken on a 5,000-mile, Soviet-sponsored journey to the newly burgeoning centers of Russian industry.

In the late 1920s Russian manpower was concentrated in the countryside. The push for industrialization required that large numbers of peasants move to the cities to build factories or dig in mines or build railroads, but at the same time the reduced agricultural population was called upon to produce much more than it had in the past via the state collective farm system. The peasants, of course, did not take kindly to this wholesale tranformation of their lives, and this "second Bolshevik revolution" eventually caused the deaths of an estimated two million to three million Russians, either from famine or outright violence.

Although at no point in her numerous talks and articles about Russia in the early thirties does Bourke-White mention this, the exciting changes and developments she observed in Russian life at that time were pervaded with terror. She was not alone in overlooking the climate of coercion that existed there. Most liberal writers and intellectuals then saw the mood of Soviet society as one of exhilaration; their attention was focused on what Harold J. Laski called "the large human goals" of "the greatest social experiment in history."

George Bernard Shaw, on the other hand, who also toured the Soviet Union in the early thirties, did not flinch from reporting the grim truth. "A considerable share of the secret of the success of Russian Communism consists in the fact that every Russian knows that if he will not make his life a paying enterprise for his country, then he will most likely lose it. An agent of the GPU will take him by the shoulder and will conduct him to the cellar of this famous department and he will simply stop living." *Pravda,* the Communist party's journal, printed his remarks without comment on May 13, 1932.

In their own way, the Russians were making industrial development the focus of their efforts during the Five-Year Plan, as the Americans had done in their own way during "the age of prosperity." The difference, of course, was that whereas the United States had shifted from an agrarian to an industrial society in a period of half a century, the Soviet Union was struggling to effect that change in one-tenth the time. Bourke-White wanted to witness and record the spirit of industry there, knowing she would find Soviet factories and the Russians' attitude toward them significantly different from what she found in the U.S. In *Eyes on Russia,* her book about her first Russian adventure, she said: "Russia to me was a land of embryo industry. . . . The industries of America are rounded out by order and efficiency. There is a certain finish to our factories. I wanted to go to Russia where all these industries would be new. I was eager to see what a factory would be like that had been plunged suddenly into being. I wanted to watch the Soviet workers put their new machinery together. But more than that I wanted to observe these agricultural people who were striving to become industrialists. Men who had left the plow for the punch press—how did they behave?"

Although Bourke-White knew she was not engaging in a scientific study of Soviet society, she did feel that her photographs would aid in understanding the Russians because she worked under the romantic assumption that in an industrial age, "if one understands the industry of a people, one comes close to the heart of that people."

» These Bolshevik factory hands, I sensed, would not be like the American worker, who takes his machinery as he takes his daily bread. There would be a consciousness of the physical appearance of the machine. There would undoubtedly be clumsy, fumbling, fitful attempts to use it. But their machinery, so hard won, would have meaning. Would carry the symbolism of power. There would be a consciousness of its shining surface, the rhythm of its gear wheels, its structural pattern. The machine would have form in their eyes. «

The one great paradox in Bourke-White's Soviet experience is that she closed her eyes to the political ramifications of a phenomenon that was intrinsically political. She went so far as to say in a 1932 radio interview that she had "walked into a situation where the whole government felt as I did. The whole body of Soviet officials believed there was beauty in industry." Bourke-White continues in that interview: "What their political ideas were I did not care, I didn't know much about it and I did not pay much attention."

Although she may have been politically naïve at that early stage in her career, she did not remain so. Discussing her Soviet experience in *Portrait of Myself*, Bourke-White explains: "To me politics were colorless beside the drama of the machine. It was only much later that I discovered that politics could be an absorbing subject with a profound effect on human destiny."

Despite the deficiencies in Bourke-White's awareness when she went to Russia in the early thirties, her photographer's instincts generally aimed her in the right direction. There is also some question as to whether Bourke-White knew more than she let on in order to maintain the good graces of the Soviet government for the purpose of making subsequent journeys to Russia.

Bourke-White knew things were "happening in Russia, and happening with staggering speed." She felt she could not afford to miss any of the changes. "I wanted to make pictures of this astonishing development, because, whatever the outcome, whether success or failure, the effort of 150,000,000 people is so gigantic, so unprecedented in all history, that I felt that these photographic records might have some historical value. I saw the Five-Year Plan as a great drama being unrolled before the eyes of the world."

Her ticket to that drama was paid for, in part, by *Fortune*. The magazine had assigned her and Parker Lloyd-Smith to cover German industry in the summer of 1930. Plans for the trip had been set early in the year. They were to begin with the North German Lloyd shipping docks and go on through the Ruhr Valley to the Allgemeine Elektrizitäts Gesellschaft (AEG), "the General Electric of Germany."

From there they proceeded to Babelsberg and the movie lots of UFA (center of the German film industry), and then on to Leuna, where Bourke-White would be the first woman ever allowed inside the secret walls of the I. G. Farben Industrie, the largest German chemical and dye corporation. There was an ominous expression current in the thirties about I. G. Farben: "If you turn left you get fertilizer, if you turn right you get poison gas." Bourke-White and Lloyd-Smith were also supposed to visit the Krupp steel works, but they failed to get permission. Only when the Ruhr fell in World War II did Bourke-White get into Krupp to photograph the ruins.

Russia interested Bourke-White's *Fortune* editors, but they doubted whether the Soviet authorities would permit her to photograph industrial subjects. When *Fortune* refused to sponsor her trip beyond the required work she was scheduled to do in Germany, Bourke-White decided to forge on into the Soviet Union at her own risk.

Tourist routes to Russia were not yet established, so Bourke-White sought the advice of people who had been there before. One of those she asked was Karl Bickel, then president of United Press International, who gave her a great deal of help. She recounts in *Eyes on Russia* that Bickel warmly encouraged her to go: "Russia is the most interesting country in the world just now," he told her. "You will be well received. The Russians love photographers. . . . In fact, they will, perhaps, receive you like a second Messiah because you are glorifying the machine." Bickel also put her in touch with the head of the Soviet Information Bureau in Washington, D.C., with whom she made an appointment for the very next day.

The head of the Soviet Information Bureau felt that it was "a fine thing" she was going to Russia. He promised to write to the All-Russian Publishing House (Gosizdat) and suggest that they use her photographs of Russian industry in their magazines. "Your photographs will appeal to the Russians," he said; "they have the Russian style." He also went so far as to arrange a meeting for her with Sergei Eisenstein, who was in New York on his way to Hollywood, so that she might show the great movie director her photographs.

Before she left Washington that evening, Bourke-White had photographed President Hoover, who received her fresh after signing the Hawley-Smoot Tariff Act, and she also met with William Green, then President of the American Federation of

Wheat field and smokestacks in the Ruhr Valley, Germany, 1930.

Labor, which occasionally bought her industrial photographs for use in their newsletters. The midnight train out of Union Station carried Bourke-White back to New York, and the next day she had a talk with the Soviet cinema genius.

Eisenstein spoke fluent English, Bourke-White wrote, "accentuated by vivid gestures." Before their talk was over he had given her letters of introduction to artists in Berlin, Paris, and Moscow, all of which he wrote himself in German, French, and Russian.

In late June 1930 Bourke-White sailed to Europe on the SS *Bremen* with Parker Lloyd-Smith and his mother. Arriving at Bremerhaven, she started work for the *Fortune* story on German industry immediately and proceeded smoothly except for one incident: Bourke-White was arrested under suspicion of being a French spy. She had been taking pictures of a wheat field in the Ruhr, showing the distant skyline of smokestacks through the wheat stalks. Unfortunately for her, the German police felt that any woman with a camera had to be a spy (there was considerable tension during that period over Alsace-Lorraine); but none of the police could question Bourke-White in English, and after being detained for eight hours she was released.

Meanwhile, Bourke-White continued to wait for her visa from Moscow. The Russian consul in Berlin had received no communication about her. But delays in receiving visas were not uncommon, and Bourke-White continued her interesting work, hoping that the delay would not be excessive in her case.

She comments on that waiting period in *Eyes on Russia* that "the days went by happily." She was delighted with the earnest bald-headed German workmen. "Their shaved egg-shaped skulls took the highlights from my thousand-watt floodlights beau-

tifully. . . ." It also amused her to find that the German workers all looked exactly alike: "they all had the same expression on their faces." She spent her nights exploring "the intricacies of Berlin's remarkable nightclubs." The elaborately mirrored dance floors, for which Berlin's nightclubs were famous, "helped for a time to keep my mind off the ever-gnawing fear that I might not be admitted into Russia."

Finally, after nearly five weeks and no word of her visa, "the days of photographing bald workers and arranging compositions with light and shadow on the turbines were filled with worry. The evenings spent tangoing in the mirrored Casanova or telephoning hilarious messages from table to table at the Femina lost their flavor."

By the end of July, with all of her work for *Fortune* completed, Bourke-White knew that she could not stay much longer in Europe. One night she could not sleep. She wandered around Berlin's Unter den Linden "in a fog of suspense and doubt." At daybreak, while walking back to her hotel, "as uninterested in the world and as discouraged" as she had ever been, she wandered near the Soviet Embassy, where the consul saw her from an upstairs window, whistled, and waved a telegram. It was the message she had been waiting for, granting her permission to enter the USSR as a photographer.

An American journalist who had just returned to Berlin from Russia told Bourke-White that American travelers in Russia fell ill for a few weeks until they became adjusted to the poor quality of Russian victuals. Because she had too much to do she could not afford to fall ill, and she therefore followed the American correspondent's order to buy a cheap trunk and fill it with canned food. In *Eyes on Russia*, Bourke-White recounts how a German *haus-*

frau friend of hers helped her buy those supplies: "Buy a sausage, but not a Christian sausage," her friend told her, "because Jewish sausages keep better than Christian sausages." Bourke-White also stocked up on cheese, chocolate, tinned fruit, and canned baked beans to help her maintain body and soul during her stay in Russia.

Buying film supplies posed an unusual last-minute problem. Days in advance of her departure she had ordered one-hundred dozen sheets of panchromatic cut film 5 inches x 7 inches. The supply store assured her the film was in stock and that the film would be ready despite such short notice. But a few hours before she was planning to leave, the store telephoned her again to report that, unfortunately for her, the continental-size film (13 centimeters x 16 centimeters) was just a fraction larger than the corresponding American size in inches. She was unable to buy enough German film holders to replace the thirty American ones she had brought. Calls to photographic suppliers in Paris, London, Munich, and Vienna failed to locate either the right size films or new film holders. But she was finally able to persuade the Berlin supply store to keep its factory open one entire night and slice the edges off a thousand sheets of film to fit the standard American format she used.

Her certificate from the Soviet Embassy in Berlin secured her against any inspection, which was a big relief because with her voluminous baggage she would have had a lot of explaining to do when her train reached the Russian-Polish border. At the first stop over the border a group of young men and women came out to the train singing the rousing melody of the "Internationale." The exhilaration of that moment disappeared the next morning, however, when Bourke-White found herself on the platform of the Moscow train station with her cameras, food supplies, and films piled around her and no taxis in sight. No taxis would come for her either. She later learned that the Soviet Union's few working automobiles were so precious that they had to be engaged days in advance. Finally, a friendly Russian girl helped her hail down two droshkies (horse-drawn carriages). Bourke-White's equipment filled the two droshkies; she herself was placed atop one of them, and all were wheeled to the Grand Hotel.

At the hotel, Bourke-White was registered into a high narrow room which reverberated with the sound of hammering from outside. The porter brought up her trunks and then, before turning to leave, spoke a few words to the Soviet correspondent who was acting as Bourke-White's interpreter. The porter's words were simple enough, but to Bourke-White he seemed to be taking personal responsibility for his whole struggling nation. "Tell the Amerikanka that things are not very good now," he said. "Tell her that we are sorry things are so poor, but if she will come back in five years everything will be better."

The first Russian official to receive Bourke-White was Leonid Petrovich Serebriakoff, vice-commissar of railways. He told her that she could be of great service to the Soviet Union, that her pictures were just what the Russians needed, and that Khalatoff, the president of the All-Russian Publishing House (Gosizdat) should see her pictures at once.

Khalatoff came in to Serebriakoff's office for a viewing of Bourke-White's photographs of American blast furnaces, oil derricks, locomotives, and coal freighters, and the two commissars discussed which Soviet industrial sites Bourke-White could photograph. Bourke-White carefully noted the scrutiny the two government men gave to her pictures. She detected a radically different attitude to her work from the one to which she was accustomed: "To the American businessman, photography or art-work of any kind is simply an instrument that crosses his consciousness once a month when his advertising manager comes around with layouts for him to O.K. But the Russians are an innately artistic people. They consider the artist an important factor in the Five-Year Plan, and the photographer the artist of the machine age. It is for the artist to stir the imagination of the people with the grandeur of the industrial program. Thus I had come to a country where an industrial photographer is accorded the rank of artist and prophet."

When the meeting was over, Serebriakoff told Bourke-White that she would be made the guest of the Soviet government with all her expenses paid, and the government would help in every possible way to accomplish her purpose. But several days passed before Serebriakoff's words were put into action. "Day after tomorrow" became a bureaucratic litany. The delays and postponements of her big trip were exasperating, and because she only had five weeks to achieve a great deal, she was determined to take some pictures in Moscow, where she could photograph bread factories, workers' clubs, textile mills, and the like.

She was escorted through the textile mill by

George Melnichanski, head of the All-Union Textile Syndicate. Melnichanski had lived for a while as a watchmaker in the United States, but returned to Russia to participate in the 1917 revolution. The first thing he asked Bourke-White was how things were in America. "We hear that the unemployment situation is terrible and that there are food lines in the New York streets. Is it true? In the Soviet Union there is no unemployment. Everybody has a job. It is only in a capitalist country that such industrial disasters can befall."

Bourke-White quotes this statement, but reserves comment. As when she compares the United States businessman's attitude toward industrial photography to that of the Russian businessman's, she lets the suggestion linger that maybe the Russian outlook on some things was superior to the American way: more enlightened, more humane. She also generalizes about the difference between the American and Russian worker, with regard to their understanding of photogenic qualities:

» Posing American workmen for photographs is often very difficult.... The minute an American worker sees a camera he becomes self-conscious. Often I have to work over every detail of his posture, changing the slope of his back, the attitude of his head, the position of every finger, until movement will be suggested by his attitude in the photograph, even though he must be photographed standing still. If he becomes too difficult to work with, I tell him to go on working while I visit another part of the factory. When he has limbered up I return, and begin over again.

But in Russia, every worker that I chose for a model acted as though he had been trained behind footlights. The Russians are a naturally dramatic people. My ignorance of Russian was no hindrance, for at a mere gesture from me they fell naturally into dramatic and expressive attitudes.... The Russians seemed to understand instinctively that I was composing a picture. With a natural eye to pictorial effect they seemed to comprehend that every detail was important in the building up of an artistic whole. «

———

The Russians were also responsive to what she had to say about her photographic work. The editor of a popular illustrated weekly newspaper that circulated throughout Russia exhorted her to address a group of editors, artists, and photographers about the art of photographing the machine. Interpreters were brought in and Bourke-White was given what was surely one of her first opportunities to lecture about her experiences and ideas with respect to photography. "You must not make a picture unusual just because you decide arbitrarily to make it unusual. You must not strain for an effect," she said. "The effect must be a natural result of your manner of expression."

She abhorred the kind of photography that "blurs over the subject with a lot of soft focus tricks and calls itself artistic." A photograph, she said, "should look like itself. It is a direct and expressive medium and it should be used for what it is." It was "an outstanding means of expression," the best, she believed, "for portraying the power and force of industry." Bourke-White concluded her talk with a summing up of her aesthetic *Weltanschauung*: "Any great art that may come out of this industrial age, will rise from industrial subjects which are powerful and sincere and close to the heart of life." With that she rose to leave, but questions from the audience followed her out the door. "What are American photographers doing? Did the workers form photographic clubs? Did their photographs portray the class struggle? Did their clubs further the victorious uprooting of capitalism?" and many other equally difficult questions for Bourke-White to answer.

Personal questions came up also, and those were another matter. How did she spend her evenings? How old was she? Did she have any boyfriends? All of which her interpreter parried by replying, "Miss Bourke-White loves nothing but her camera."

Although the red tape and bureaucracy seemed impermeable, the gate was opened wide one day in August, when the treasurer of Gosizdat handed Bourke-White a fat roll of ruble notes to pay expenses for herself and her interpreter on a five-thousand-mile journey. She was to visit Dnieperstroi, where Colonel Hugh Cooper, the American engineer who built the Roosevelt Dam and Muscle Shoals, was superintending the construction of the world's largest dam over the Dnieper River. From there she would go to Rostov, where the largest collective farms were being developed; after that she would start south for Novorossisk, a seaport on the Black Sea where the oldest and largest cement factory in the Soviet Union was located; and thence a long trip to Stalingrad on the Volga. Stalingrad had once been an overgrown village called Tsaritsyn, but

In Russia, 1932.

when the village acquired industry it also got Stalin's name. That city was the highlight of the trip for Bourke-White because she planned to visit the steel plant that was being enlarged there to supply metal for a new tractor factory, Tractorstroi. She wanted to photograph Tractorstroi most of all, she said, because there she could observe how the Russians behaved in a thoroughly Americanized industry, operated along American lines and supervised by American engineers. She had visited similar industries in the United States and expected Tractorstroi to give her a chance to make comparisons.

Eyes on Russia is filled with anecdotes about the sites Bourke-White visited. All of the stories she tells illuminate in some way the character of the young Soviet Republic and the manner in which the Five-Year Plan was carried out. She recounts, for example, the story of the Russians' early experiences operating the giant American cranes to build Dnieperstroi: "It seems that at first the Russians believed that cranes could lift anything and everything: Ac-

cording to one story, the workers at Dnieperstroi tried to pull down a thousand-ton boulder with a locomotive crane; according to another, half the cranes brought over during the first six months of their use were busy lifting up the other half which had been overturned by naïve workers seeking to achieve miracles."

Bourke-White met Hugh Cooper at the site of the great dam, then the largest in the world, and made her famous portrait of him standing in front of the giant earthworks. Then she proceeded by train to Verblud, a large state collective farm, and during the long ride Bourke-White and her interpreter-guide, Lida Ivanovna, compared the differences in their life-styles. Lida Ivanovna wanted to know what Bourke-White paid for dresses and shoes, and Bourke-White carefully explained the range between Gimbels' prices and Bergdorf Goodman's. Their talk then turned to the subject of food.

Lida Ivanovna wanted to know what apple pie was. "I made a sketch to explain this," Bourke-White wrote, "and descriptions of apple pie lead to descriptions of Eskimo Pie, the thought of which thrilled both of us."

Bourke-White and her guide subsisted for days on the remaining canned rations in Bourke-White's trunk. The variety of foods she had brought from Berlin was quickly reduced to a great reserve of canned beans, and the two women sustained themselves almost exclusively on beans for days at a time.

Then Lida Ivanovna asked why American women dieted and what they ate when they were dieting. Bourke-White explained in *Eyes on Russia* that "Several years of climbing scaffolds on skyscrapers under construction, of swinging down cranes in steel mills, and scrambling up piers of bridges had turned my thoughts to other subjects than that of dieting, and I was therefore unable to give her very full information." Lida Ivanovna wanted Bourke-White especially to confirm that all American women were thin; wanted to know what food cost, what an American ate in a typical day, and what time Americans took their meals. "What time do you eat in Russia?" Bourke-White asked. "When we have food," replied Lida Ivanovna.

At Verblud, Bourke-White had her first real meal in days, a breakfast of roast pork and mashed potatoes, followed by two soft-boiled eggs. She described the experience in terms befitting an epiphany: "Were those the sounds of eggshells cracking gently open, or cherubim and seraphim singing in the distance? The speed with which egg and pork can be turned into zeal and energy was something I had not noticed in my own country where the cafeteria and lunchroom lurk around every corner."

When they got to Novorossisk to photograph the cement factory, a delegation of local editors called on Bourke-White in her hotel. The editors examined her photographs, but were fascinated most of all with her official papers, which were covered with all manner and color of stamps and seals. "With such papers," Bourke-White quotes the reporters as saying, "the young lady could travel to the moon." Soon the meeting settled down to business. The editors asked many probing questions: "Who achieves the highest rate of production, the American factory or the Russian factory?"

"I was frightened," Bourke-White wrote. "My replies were important. They would undoubtedly appear at great length in print." So she equivocated. "Both the American factory and the Russian factory achieve a high rate of production," she answered warily, and Lida Ivanovna expanded that reply for twenty minutes. Next: Is the Russian worker as efficient as the American worker? Lida Ivanovna talked for three-quarters of an hour. "Which does the American photo-correspondent prefer to photograph, the American worker or the Russian worker?"

"The American worker and the Russian worker both have very interesting faces," Bourke-White replied, and with that scant material her interpreter developed an endless answer until finally, approving and satisfied at last, the interviewers rose to go home.

Bourke-White was most curious to find out what opinions she had expressed to the press, and when the last bowing editor left the room, Lida Ivanovna told her that she had said, "Miss Bourke-White loved to photograph the Russian workers, that she found great character in these energetic faces, that she preferred to photograph the Russian worker because his face had such individuality. I told the editors that Miss Bourke-White much prefers the Soviet worker to the American worker because the American worker has no individuality. In America the workman performs one operation always. In America the workman is chained to mass production. In America the workman is a puppet, an automaton. Miss Bourke-White loves much better to photograph the Russian worker because in America the workman is nothing but a machine."

Like it or not, Bourke-White was being used as propaganda, but she evidently felt that the exploitation was mutual. Letting the government put words in her mouth was a reasonable and somewhat amusing sacrifice to make for receiving the government's generous help in photographing Soviet industry.

As Bourke-White explains in *Portrait of Myself*, she was not the only American who had made arrangements with the government:

» There was virtually a little Cleveland within Soviet borders. Warner & Swasey and Foote-Burt were tooling up Stalingrad. Two of Cleveland's leading construction companies, McKee and Austin, built some of the biggest installations in the Soviet Union—from steel mills in Siberia to oil refineries on the Black Sea.

Detroit, too, was prominently represented by Ford; Schenectady by General Electric. Ford's industrial architect, Albert Kahn, was laying out the entire group of factory buildings for Stalingrad.... The Newport News Shipbuilding Company was furnishing what were then the world's largest hydroturbines for Dnieperstroi.... These great American builders and their staffs of engineers and planners were not, of course, dangerous Reds, or even fellow travelers. They were not working for ideological or propaganda purposes, but strictly for business reasons or—as the Marxists might have said—"the profit motive." The role played by American industrialists in building up the Soviet giant cannot be overestimated. **«**

———

Tractorstroi, the Stalingrad tractor factory that Bourke-White was interested in photographing, was built under American John Calder's supervision in one year by 6,200 Russian workers who had little or no experience in heavy construction. The first tractor had come off the assembly line just two months before Bourke-White's arrival in Moscow, but many manufacturing problems had still to be ironed out when Bourke-White visited the plant. Bourke-White explained in a slide lecture that the Russians had a curious attitude toward their machines: "They are so new and wonderful to them that they are like children marveling over new toys. They make speeches about the machine, make posters about it, talk about it and discuss the machine, but they do not know how to operate it." One of the American engineers' chief complaints was that it seemed that no sooner did they get a job started when their men went off to smoke cigarettes. The women, on the other hand, seldom took their smokes, Bourke-White pointed out. The women were generally more earnest about their work, she said; they learned their machines faster, and took their jobs more seriously than the men did.

Bourke-White's tour through Tractorstroi was as illuminating as she had hoped it would be with regard to the differences between American and Soviet factories. She was impressed above all with the Russian capacity to learn quickly, although she knew the vast industrial program they were embarking upon could not be accomplished in five years. There was, in fact a second Five-Year Plan, lasting from 1934 to 1939, in which her friend Serebriakoff was purged, along with many others whom Stalin considered enemies of the state. In 1930, however, Bourke-White knew nothing about purges. The phenomenon that riveted her attention, as in the United States, was the making of steel, which she witnessed and recorded in Stalingrad at the Red October plant. Her description of the pouring of the molten heat stands out as one of her best pieces of writing.

» As we made our way to the open hearth a column of smoke rose into the sky. A furnace had just been tapped, and 100 tons of gleaming metal were flowing into the ladle. Sparks streaking through the air, dancing on the floor, smoke in orange gusts bursting above the liquid steel.

The next heat would be poured in twenty minutes. There was no time to lose. I snatched the straps off of my equipment cases, drew out my thousand-watt bulbs, screwed them into their mogul sockets, and set the reflectors on pedestals. Two of the factory electricians raced away with my cables to make connections while I set up my tripod. I scanned the jumbled floor, littered with slag lumps and castaway ingot molds, for vantage-points for the lamps. A shout from the electricians. "They want you to throw on the switch," called my interpreter. The instant's worry for fear the circuit might be overloaded and the fuses give way. On with the switch. A flood of light. The fuses hold. That hurdle taken.

From the dark recesses of the factory a crane swings into sight, bringing the ladle to set it for the next heat. The crane clatters into position above us. The suspending ropes lengthen and the huge ladle is lowered gradually into place....

I had four minutes to decide where to place my floodlights to the best advantage, and what viewpoint to choose for my camera. The open hearth had been constructed in a curious way with only half a roof. Counting on the daylight which streamed from the open end, I studied the heaviest shadows, and placed my lights as close to the black side of the ladle as I dared, allowing leeway for probable splashes of metal which would blow out my bulbs if it reached them. I spared a few precious seconds to step back on a lump of slag and survey the black side of the ladle through half-closed eyes, making sure that my lights would pick out the heavy bolts, which would give the photographed ladle form and structure.

The work on the floor accomplished, I glanced at the furnace above me. Workmen were pummeling at the mouth of the furnace, and at the correct instant when the steel reached the right heat for pouring they would draw out the plug. Not a minute to lose. I snatched an armful of holders, threw my camera over my shoulder, and started up the nearest ladder to the roof.

A cross-beam, wide enough for me to walk on but just too narrow to place a camera steadily. A spurt of smoke from the furnace. Soon it would be beginning. I waved and shouted to the crane operator. He understood me and shot his crane down to a point within reach. I handed him my instrument gingerly, followed it with the filmholders, reached for the greasy suspension ropes with both hands, and slipped into the crane cab. Just time enough to set up the camera in my cramped space, before hell rushed forth beneath my feet.

A drunken orgy of metal, a living whiteness welling upward, flames dancing across its surface, sparks driven out like bullets. I ducked beneath my camera cloth and took my focus, placed my filmholder, and with my hand upon the shutter was just about to take the picture when the smoke condensed beneath us, hiding the whole scene as the earth is hidden from an aviator by a cloud. The smoke thinned away. I began to shoot. Placing filmholders, removing slides, pushing the trigger, counting the seconds, watching the camera for steadiness, studying the flow of the metal, placing more holders, counting more seconds. Until, at last, the difficulty that I dreaded set in. The crane cab began trembling as though with palsy. Every movement now must be a supreme economy. The length of my exposure must depend, not upon my judgment as a photographer, but upon the brief respite allowed me when the crane quieted for a moment and the camera became steady. Exposure after exposure, in an agony of fear that the camera was not still. A hundred plates, in the hope that one would be perfect.

The heavy stream slowed down, dwindling from the thickness of a tree trunk to the thickness of a man's arm; a last pinwheel of sparks; the metal rose to the edge of the ladle like turgid soup, white heat became red heat, and the slag crept to the top of the flowing crater, mottling the surface, orange against gold. «

On the last day of her sojourn in Moscow, Bourke-White worked like mad to develop the 800 negatives she had exposed on her trip, in order that the Soviet censors might clear them for leaving the country. She stayed up for thirty-six hours without sleep, working with a Soviet technician and Lida Ivanovna in a small motion picture studio darkroom. Luckily, Bourke-White had brought with her a piece of green glass from Berlin. Her panchromatic films could only be developed under green light and the glass was unavailable in Moscow.

In one night the three co-workers processed the 800 films. All were spread around the floor in trays of hypo, and all day Bourke-White knelt on her knees in front of the bathtub in her hotel rinsing the films; and throughout the night that followed she carefully hung up the delicate emulsions to dry.

» The night dragged on like an endless nightmare. Dazed with lack of sleep, I stood on a chair, put pins through films and films on cords, pins through films and films on cords, until dawn broke. Morning found my ceiling black with the fluttering images of cement kilns, dams, state farms, socialized horses, spectacled iron puddlers, tractors and textiles. Exhausted and triumphant, I threw myself on the bed and, under the gentle rain of films dripping from the ceiling, I at once fell asleep. «

Bourke-White returned to Berlin by train, after leaving her films with the Soviet censorship authorities and picking up a sixteenth-century ikon, which she wrapped in a sweater at the bottom of her suitcase to avoid inspection at the border. One of the biggest shocks she experienced on her trip back to "civilization" was when she saw a well-stocked delicatessen in Warsaw: "I looked through the window eagerly, finding it hard to accustom myself to a display of so much food. Here, if I wished, I could walk into the store and buy anything. No government papers would be needed. There would be no waiting in a queue."

She traveled on to Berlin and then to Paris in a continued state of shock because "porters, costumers, couturiers, concierges were ready to do everything to accommodate visitors." She found she had to check herself, when a maid cleaned up her room or a porter brought a parcel, from saying, "Thank you, comrade!"

Sergei Eisenstein having a shave on the terrace of Margaret Bourke-White's studio, 1930.

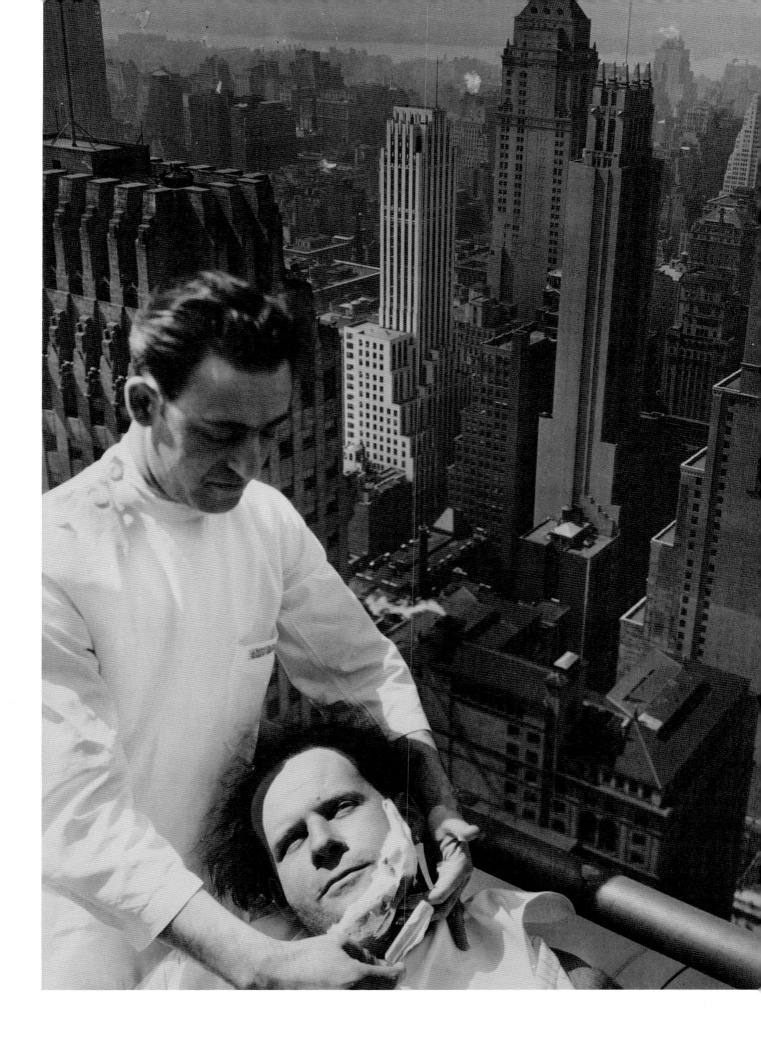

Butcher, Germany, 1931.

Workmen in the AEG plant, Germany, 1930.

40

Electrazavod, USSR, 1930.

Tractorstroi, USSR, 1930.

Dam at Dnieperstroi, USSR, 1930.

Magnitogorsk, USSR, 1931.

Ballet school students, Moscow, 1931.

Magnitogorsk, USSR, 1931.

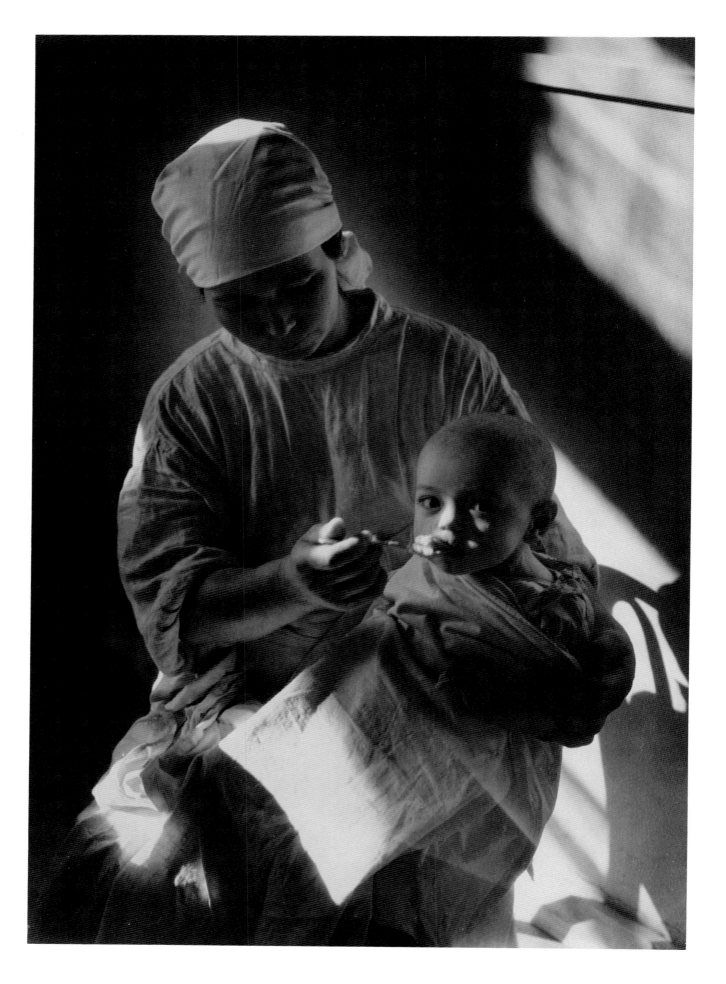

Moscow nursery, 1931.

Mother and child, USSR, 1932.

Marina Semyonova, leading ballerina of the Moscow Opera, 1931.

Machine dance, Moscow Ballet School, 1931.

German army on maneuvers, 1932.

General Hans von Seeckt, Germany, 1932.

On November 30, 1930, about two months after she returned from the Soviet Union, Bourke-White moved her studio from the Terminal Tower in Cleveland to the tower of the Chrysler Building in New York City. She had learned the space was available while on assignment for Chrysler, photographing the construction of their new skyscraper. Her photographs had to prove that the tower was an integral part of the building, not just an ornament, because if it were just an ornament Chrysler would be unable to claim that their 1,046-foot-tall building was the highest in the world.

On the sixty-first floor Bourke-White discovered that there were stainless steel gargoyles jutting out at the four corners. These were the deciding factor for her; no other location would be satisfactory, and Bourke-White immediately went about trying to get a lease. *Fortune* interceded on her behalf when the landlords expressed reluctance about renting such prime space to a woman. They thought she would surely get married before too much time went by and forget about her photography business. But Bourke-White finally obtained a lease, and applied for the janitor's job. She wanted to live in her studio, and by law only the janitor of an office building was allowed to live in it. Although she did not get the job, Bourke-White frequently worked throughout the night in her studio.

The studio had a pair of the gargoyles, which she named Min and Bill. Bourke-White also had a large terrace outside her studio, for giving parties, and a small terrace, where she kept two pet alligators (Mercury and Mars), which a friend had sent her from Florida. Eight turtles kept company with the alligators.

The inside of Bourke-White's studio was equally exotic, from an urban standpoint. John Vassos designed custom-built furniture for the room. Everything from the built-in bookshelves to the cabinet for her radio set was hand-crafted, and the studio was transformed into a masterpiece of art-deco design. Although pieces constructed of wood were prominent, Vassos installed aluminum and glass tables and chairs, and the light fixtures all concealed their bulbs behind rectangular boxes of frosted glass. One of the room's outstanding features was its warm raspberry rug. Bourke-White felt it was the most beautiful studio in the world, besides being the highest, and she was not alone in thinking this. *Architectural Forum* magazine was sufficiently impressed by

Margaret Bourke-White's studio in the Chrysler Building, 1930.

the studio's design to give it an article illustrated with several photographs in its January 1932 issue.

From her lofty headquarters, Bourke-White directed a photography business that increased its gross sales to nearly $30,000 in 1931, prospering during a particularly grim period in the American economy. She did a great deal of advertising photography, published *Eyes on Russia*, and devoted several months to *Fortune* stories.

But in the summer of 1931 she took off again for another adventure in the Soviet Union. Arriving in Moscow for the second time, Bourke-White was determined not to repeat difficulties she had experienced the previous summer in developing her films, and the first thing she did was find a hotel room with a bathtub. The delays and red tape of her previous year's visit were over. In fact, the Soviets thought so highly of her that they loaned her an automobile and driver for the duration of her stay in Moscow.

The use of a car and a bathtub, plus her prior acquaintance with Moscow, enabled Bourke-White to do an enormous amount of work. She would rise at 5:30 A.M., develop films for two hours on her knees beside the bathtub, and eat breakfast while shifting films. The food had improved greatly since 1930. Although she had packed canned goods for her journeys out of the city, the hotel in Moscow supplied her with breakfasts of fried eggs, stewed fruit, black bread, and Russian coffee and equally substantial dinners in the evening when she returned from her vigorous day's work. After dinner she would return to the bathtub to sponge the films left under running water all day, and hang them up to dry.

During her 1931 trip Bourke-White carefully observed aspects of Russian life that had little to do with industrial phenomena for a six-part series of articles on Russia that appeared in *The New York Times Sunday Magazine* between February and September 1932. In order to define Soviet life for the general public she knew she had to view it from many different angles, had to be more of a sociologist than she had been on her first trip.

Bourke-White took guidance, of course, from the *Times* editors, who knew what they wanted a series on Russia to include. But the insights into the new Russia that appeared in the series are Bourke-White's own, and she also incorporated her experiences in public lectures.

One of the subjects that greatly interested Bourke-White was the Russian nursery: "The work of the women in the factories is made possible by the nurseries," she pointed out in a 1932 lecture. She said that they were "bright sunshiny places," that the Soviets took great care of their children, and that children were given "every possible advantage." Bourke-White was quick to point out that the nursery was, above all, a place of education, not only for children, but for mothers as well.

It amused Bourke-White to learn that for the Russians "culture" meant cleanliness and health care. If mothers brought their children to the nurseries in dirty clothes the children would be undressed outside the door, handed through the door, dressed in clean clothes by the nursery for the day, and dressed in their home clothes and handed out through the door again when their mothers came and collected them at night.

Bourke-White also looked into the Moscow ballet school that year and found one of the best demonstrations of how industry was pervading Russian life during the Five-Year Plan. Machine dances, which carried out the motions of gear wheels, pistons, and screws, were being designed. "The Soviets send choreographers to the factories," Bourke-White explained. "Specialists will go to a textile factory and study the interweaving of threads and the motions of the spools and use these forms in designing a dance. An airplane dance has been designed which shows the slow motion of the plane at the beginning, its accelerated motion as it drives across the field and ends with movements which indicate the rise of the airplane into the air."

Bourke-White also took note of the new form of workers' drama that was emerging in Moscow. "It was largely an educational play, but very amusing," she said of a skit about the Five-Year Plan entitled "Tempo." One of the actors represented John Calder, the American engineer who had been appointed coordinator of construction for the entire Soviet Union; the other actors represented bricklayers. The theme, of course, was productivity—how to finish the Five-Year Plan in four years.

In 1931 the most amazing construction work Bourke-White photographed was Magnitogorsk, a new steel-making city being developed in the Ural Mountains under the direction of ubiquitous John Calder.

Calder told Bourke-White many stories about the blundering, inexperienced Russian workers on whom he had to rely to carry out the job. Bourke-White wondered why, if the Russians had so little training, there were so few fatal accidents and Calder said he guessed it was because God was with the Bolsheviks.

Apparently God was also with Bourke-White on her suspense-filled journey to Magnitogorsk. The city was located in the most inaccessible part of the Urals, on the edge of Siberia. Going by train would have taken a week, and because she could not sacrifice so much time, Bourke-White decided to go by airplane, a two-day flight.

Bourke-White spent five days in Magnitogorsk, covering various facets of the activities going on there. Her government sponsorship gave her the unusual power to stop workers in their tracks, if necessary. "I was delighted to see a group of peasants dragging a log up the mountainside. They made a marvelous sound, not singing, but a rhythmic sound which coordinated with their rhythmic movements. I stopped them to take the pictures and they were very good natured while I made my exposure, but as soon as I had completed the photograph, with no self-consciousness, the rhythmic chant went on again."

When Bourke-White returned to Moscow to develop her photographs, she found she had made more exposures than her remaining chemicals would process. She had brought sufficient supplies with her, of course, but her "comrade" the chambermaid had unknowingly poured many of her chemicals down the sink. There was very little hypo left. There was hypo in Russia, but so little of it that it could not be bought in the stores. She could have obtained some hypo through her official connections, but feared that the red tape would hold her up for days. Since she had to return to America without delay she cabled a reporter friend of hers in Berlin who located five pounds of hypo for her there, and took the package to the Soviet Ambassador in Berlin. The hypo was then delivered in a diplomatic pouch to Moscow, where a squad of soldiers picked it up and carried it to Bourke-White's hotel.

Bourke-White returned to America in November 1931 when the country's industrial economy, in startling contrast to the overall economic progress Bourke-White had witnessed in the Soviet Union, seemed hopelessly paralyzed.

The six articles Bourke-White wrote for *The New York Times*, which were lavishly illustrated with her photographs, went a long way toward informing the American public about the more positive aspects of life in Russia.

Bourke-White's "scoop" with photographs of the Five-Year Plan in action riveted a great deal of public attention. "Silk Stockings in the Five-Year Plan," the first article to appear (on February 14, 1932), was a portrait of Soviet womanhood. "Making Communists of Soviet Children" was the second in the series (March 6, 1932). "Nothing Bores the Russian Audience" (March 13, 1932) was a review of public entertainment and culture in the USSR. "Where the Worker Can Drop the Boss" (March 27, 1932) showed how different from American attitudes was the whole concept of work in the Soviet Union. "A Day's Work for the Five-Year Plan" (May 22, 1932) was a portrait of Miloff, a Magnitogorsk bricklayer. Bourke-White followed him throughout one entire working day—from the moment he woke up in his barracks until the end of the workday at three o'clock, when the workers were assembled for a group meeting, and on until the end of the day, when Miloff retired for the night, dreaming of the bathtubs he had heard they will be installing in the new workers' homes outside of Magnitogorsk in "Socialist City." "To have a bathtub," Miloff exclaims, "how cultural that will be!" "A Day in a Remote Village of Russia" (September 11, 1932) provided a rare view of how the Russian Revolution was sweeping away old ways of life. Bourke-White used the village of Vertne Uralsky, located at the foothills of the Urals, as an exemplar of the changing conditions in small villages all over the Soviet Union.

The articles brought Bourke-White considerable personal attention. She did numerous radio interviews, her byline appeared under photographs in *Vanity Fair* and other major periodicals, and she was becoming known as something of an expert on the Soviet Union.

As was the case with her *New York Times* series and with *Eyes on Russia*, which was the brainchild of her publishers, Max Schuster and Richard Simon, Bourke-White seems to have undertaken the task of expository writing only when handed an appealing opportunity.

At this stage in her life, Bourke-White preferred the directness and immediacy of public lectures and radio interviews. Directness and immediacy were also the qualities that attracted Bourke-White to cinema in the early thirties. In 1932 she wrote to a friend: "I feel that industrial moving pictures can be made with just as great artistic and dramatic value as stills, and I have been experimenting toward that end all spring, working by myself and as quietly as possible, because I wanted to explore the possibilities myself first, and be sure of my ground before I tried to place the work commercially."

In the summer of 1932 Bourke-White had gone to Rochester, New York, to talk over some technical experiments she had made with the research department of the Eastman Company. The warm reception they gave her was most gratifying: "The Eastman people have been watching my work from the very beginning since I got out of college and now that I have these ideas about movies they are deeply interested."

The Eastman people felt that the kind of movies Bourke-White would make would help fill the needs of colleges. Bourke-White believed that her movies would be used by industrial plants for publicity, but on a much wider scale. Had television been more than a gleam in an electrician's eye at that time, Bourke-White would have realized just how much wider. The Eastman people were anxious to help her in every possible way. They donated films for her continuing work with industrial motion pictures and for the film she made in Russia in 1932 as well.

In November 1932 Bourke-White brought out of the Soviet Union the first moving pictures of the Five-Year Plan that any non-Russian had been able to make on anything but an amateur scale. All the large movie companies of the time, including Pathé and Fox Movietone, had offered large sums to be allowed to make motion pictures of the Five-Year Plan and were refused. Bourke-White could hardly believe that her films were safely in her trunk.

She was unsure about the form her movies would take, and it was of utmost importance to her that the making of the film not be rushed. She had some very definite ideas about the editing of the films: "Editing (or cutting) is as important in moving pictures as the taking. In America it is usually very artlessly done in a routine manner and I want to make sure that in all my work, this and any other I may do in the future, I can supervise the editing and make sure it is done artistically as well."

Bourke-White's third consecutive summer trip to Russia, in 1932, was in many respects her most adventurous of all. Among other things, she went to the oilfields of Baku, and to the official opening of Dnieperstroi, visited some very modern kindergartens, and shot a movie of the ballet school. But the most interesting work she did that year took her to some primitive and inaccessible villages which no foreigner had ever visited before. She traveled to Tbilisi (formerly Tiflis), the capital of the Republic of Georgia in southern Russia, where the *Dovnakom*, or governing body, decided to make her the guest of the government. She was even taken off on a trip with the president of Georgia and his seven commissars through the mountain villages approaching the Turkish border, a journey which Bourke-White could not have done by herself because this was a territory forbidden to foreigners for military reasons.

"It was perhaps the most exciting trip of my life," Bourke-White wrote. "We went on horseback, had to pick our way over the steepest cliffs and mountain passes, ford rivers. At night we slept on the ground. If we were hungry, the President would order the peasants to bring a sheep which was killed and roasted over a fire as we waited. There had been fifteen escaped murderers from Turkey so our party went heavily armed."

Upon her return to Tbilisi, Bourke-White had the best coup of all from a news point of view—she took movies of Stalin's mother and the village where Stalin was born.

» Tiflis: The old palaces set in the midst of exquisite gardens. Wide balustrades and carved stairways. New home of Stalin's mother. She lives there, not in palatial luxury but in a simple two-room apartment. Rest of the palace is given over

Stalin's mother, 1932.

to the most businesslike looking of government offices. Her little apartment has no rugs on the floor. A neat white bed is set against one wall, with two tiny spotless white pillows like marshmallows placed upon it. The walls are covered with cartoons of Stalin and with photographs of two of Stalin's sons—her two favorites. The older one, about 25, the son of Stalin's first wife and the younger one, a baby, the child of Nadejda Ulli . . . the second wife who has just died. Waiting for Stalin's mother to appear I looked not only at the photographs, but underneath them as well. On the back of one of her tiny grandsons were the words written by the photographer who had printed the picture: "To the rare mother of a rare son." Stalin's mother comes into the room. She had never before met an American girl. "What was America like?" How had I had the courage to come so far? Was I married? She gave the impression of a very old woman. She had very little to say but was cordial, as all Georgians are. She came with me into the garden and I cranked my camera as she walked slowly down the curved steps of the palace. She moved with extraordinary dignity. Her face was not beautiful, but the features were well defined and the face full of character. One felt she might have been extremely beautiful when she was young. «

[Notes taken at the time and eventually incorporated into the script for her movie.]

———

Bourke-White also shot a fair number of still photographs on her 1932 summer excursion abroad. In Germany, for instance, which Bourke-White passed through on her way home, she photographed the German military forces, rearming themselves in defiance of the peace treaty that ended World War I. *Fortune* published a spread of those photographs with an article entitled "Germany's Reichswehr." At this juncture, Bourke-White was still working for *Fortune* part-time, according to the original agreement. But the excitement of the first few issues, in which Bourke-White photographs were featured almost exclusively, had abated.

In 1932 the Pennsylvania Academy of the Fine Arts exhibited a few photographs by Bourke-White in their first photography salon, and she was invited to serve on the jury for the Second Philadelphia International Salon of Photography held in May 1933. Also in 1932 the National Alliance of Art and Industry, in Washington, D.C., exhibited two of her photographs in an exhibition of one-hundred prints during the month of October. Those were but a few of the many exhibitions Bourke-White was invited to enter on the East Coast. Lloyd La Page Rollins, director of the M. H. de Young Memorial Museum in Golden Gate Park, San Francisco, exhibited a group of forty of Bourke-White's Russian pictures between February 7 and March 3, 1933. Rollins also arranged to have the exhibit travel to several museums along the West Coast that year. Those exhibits brought Bourke-White's work to the attention of Group f.64. She was personally invited to attend the opening of the Ansel Adams Gallery on Friday, September 1, 1933, a show that featured photographs by Edward Weston, Willard Van Dyke, Sonya Noskowiak, Henry Swift, Consuelo Kanaga, John Paul Edwards, Imogen Cunningham, and Ansel Adams himself. Adams and Bourke-White had met at some point in 1933, and although she would have liked to be present at the show, an important project in New York prevented her from traveling west at that time. However, she continued to stay in touch with members of that group for several years thereafter.

New York, after all, was her headquarters, and she therefore made closer ties with colleagues there and elsewhere on the East Coast. Bourke-White was also constantly deluged with invitations for speaking engagements on the East Coast. So deluged, in fact, that beginning in 1933 Bourke-White turned the handling of her speaking engagements over to the Alber & Wickes Agency, who arranged her itinerary, collected fees, and advised her on how to improve her lectures. Bourke-White was not the easiest client to handle. She had a policy of demanding that any group who hired her to speak also hire a stand-in for the same occasion, because she never knew when her advertising work or a sudden *Fortune* assignment would force her to change plans. For the most part, Bourke-White found that she could fit speaking engagements into her circuitous travels en route to various photography jobs. She spoke more often than she canceled, and therefore kept a good relationship with Alber & Wickes for several years.

Bourke-White's fame increased tremendously between 1932 and 1933, but her income shrank. Her gross sales fell to below $18,000 in 1932. The drop was due primarily to the overall decline in the United States economy. Businesses were failing left and right, and the ones able to survive had little money to spend on advertisements. Bourke-White had also been off in the Soviet Union for approximately a third of each of the three previous years— time she might have spent building her advertising accounts in an effort to hedge against possible hard times.

To try to bring her financial situation around in 1933, she launched a campaign to solicit business. She sent letters to a number of companies recommended to her by a close friend in an investment brokerage house who knew which firms were still paying for ads. Her letters provoked a brisk response, and much of Bourke-White's time in the spring and summer of 1933 was spent meeting with corporate representatives and their advertising agencies. Her notes from one of those meetings indicate the sort of work she was asked to do: "Talked about their beer account. They want at least one good photograph, perhaps a jolly butler coming in with a tray of beer."

One of the advertising agencies with which Bourke-White became associated asked her to deliver a talk about her photography to their creative staff so that they might have an informed impression of how best to put her to work. She did so on February 1, 1933. Sensitive to the needs and interests of her

Photograph for a Goodyear tire advertisement, about 1933.

audience, Bourke-White said: "The Russian Government is doing a huge selling job." "It doesn't correspond to our selling job here, but it can certainly be called advertising. There is no private trade in Russia," Bourke-White went on. "The Soviet State is selling the idea of Communism instead of religion, socialism instead of capitalism. It is selling the idea of collective instead of individual work."

To discuss Russian social propaganda in advertising terms would be unthinkable today but Bourke-White had been so warmly received on her three trips to the Soviet Union that she could not help identifying herself in a positive way with the social progress she had witnessed.

Although she was not a Communist herself, her travels and her statements caused more than a few people to wonder about her allegiance. For example, while she was in the Soviet Union in 1932, her office received an invitation to join an organization called Rebel Arts, which presented itself as an organization of artists in all fields "affiliated with or sympathetic to the Socialist and Labor movement." "In the hopes that your fine photographic work in Soviet Russia means that you are in sympathy with the radical movement," the letter began, "I am writing to ask you to join Rebel Arts. . . . Knowing that your study of modern industrial life must have led you to do some thinking along revolutionary lines, I urge you to let us know whether we can count on you."

Had Bourke-White done some thinking along "revolutionary lines"? Her statements about Soviet society and politics clearly show that she had indeed done some thinking. Her sympathies had been favorably swayed toward the Russians. But she also understood that the Soviet Union was a unique country, with a unique history and distinct social needs. As for the United States, she recognized that the country had come too far (albeit, unable to avoid some serious economic problems) and was too highly developed industrially and politically to warrant a socialist revolution on its soil. She never replied to the Rebel Arts query.

A corner of the studio, 1930.

Gargoyle outside Margaret Bourke-White's Chrysler Building studio, 1930.

Interior of a Wurlitzer organ, 1931.

Grain elevator pipes, 1932.

International Paper Company, 1933.

Detail of a Royal typewriter, 1934.

Workman in the Bethlehem Steel Corporation dry dock, Baltimore, 1935.

Signaling the hoisting of an oil tanker's forepeak bulkhead, Baltimore, 1935.

Delman shoes, about 1933.

Street in the Garment Center, New York City, 1930.

The *Vanitie* in a practice spin, Newport, 1934.

Yacht *Endeavour* at Newport, 1935.

Bourke-White's reaction to conditions in the United States had not evolved to the point of direct criticism, much less activism, in 1932. But her Soviet experiences had a significant influence and eventually did color the opinions she expressed about American life. It took witnessing the devastation of the Dust Bowl in the United States Southwest to bring her to the point of speaking out against economic and social injustice in her own country. That turning point in Bourke-White's life occurred in 1934. Until then, Bourke-White had kept her peace about America. Her mind ran toward thoughts of crisis, but on a global scale, and one of the most curious illustrations of that is a "News Note" that Max Schuster circulated in response to a conversation he and Bourke-White had had. The note is headed "Next!" and contains the following brief lines:

"Margaret Bourke-White, whose *Eyes on Russia* was published by Simon & Schuster last year, has applied to the Inner Sanctum for first rights for photographing the 'second world war.' " The news note is dated July 31, 1933!

Besides planning for World War II, Bourke-White was also talking to Hollywood during the summer of 1933. On June 28 she had a meeting with Oscar Serlin of Paramount in her New York studio. The producer wanted her to go out to Hollywood to work on one picture but suggested she wait until the right picture came along. Serlin recommended that she begin as a technical assistant and sit in on conferences to find out how everything was done, from the writing of the screenplay to the making of the sets, through the rough cut and then the final cut. Serlin also told Bourke-White it was a mistake to go into industrial pictures only. Bourke-White told Serlin she would be interested in working for the studio provided the subject of the picture interested her and she could contribute something to the film. If that was the case, she wanted very much to go.

Bourke-White also had contact with MGM in the summer of 1933. Early in July she sent David O. Selznick a massive portfolio of nearly fifty pictures made up of eight or ten smaller portfolios, each of which created its own unit, or essay, on a particular industry. Selznick was evidently considering a movie on industry that would incorporate Bourke-White's dramatic stills. The industries represented were textiles, meat packing, steel, oil, power, grain, paper,

mining, and building. Included with each portfolio was a list of captions showing how the stills could be sequenced together in a comprehensible form.

A movie constructed along the lines of her portfolios would have had the same kind of impact as a story in *Fortune* but would be more direct. Unfortunately, if movies were made from Bourke-White's industrial stills at the time, those films are no longer extant. The only movie of Bourke-White's that ever received a public showing was *Red Republic*, which when released was hardly the film Bourke-White had set out to make about her trip to the Soviet Union. Her initial goal, of course, was to supervise the editing and sound track herself in the hope of creating a documentary masterpiece on the Five-Year Plan. Besides her own footage, Bourke-White required stock footage of various scenes in the USSR that she had been unable to record herself. Sovkino, the Soviet cinema agency in New York, broke policy at her request and sold her some of their footage on the condition that Bourke-White give Sovkino a percentage of whatever she made from selling her film.

For months Bourke-White's film went without a buyer. Then in September 1933 President Roosevelt agreed to receive the Soviet Ambassador. It looked as though the United States would recognize the Soviet Union at last, and a flurry of interest in Bourke-White's movie followed. The Van Buren Company, a subsidiary of RKO, bought the film in February 1934. They paid Bourke-White $3,000 for 2,000 feet of film, including Bourke-White's voice-over narration, and those 2,000 feet of film (about one hour's worth) were edited down and released as a ten-minute short by Van Buren.

Bourke-White should have continued to recognize that her cinema experiments had sufficient historical value to warrant their preservation but that is sadly not the case. On January 5, 1938, two years after Bourke-White began working for *Life* magazine, her secretary wrote to Lloyd's Film Storage Company: "Miss Bourke-White has decided that she no longer wishes to keep her movie film and would like to know whether you are in a position to dispose of it. It can be thrown away, burned, torn up, anything you want to do with it, just so long as we are no longer carrying the expense of storage charges." The bill from Lloyd's, which came to $9.58 per month, was ten months in arrears.

The callous destruction of her cinema experiments is all the more surprising because while she was engaged in making films Bourke-White became active in two organizations devoted to the art and history of cinema: the Film Society and the Film Forum. The Film Society brought Bourke-White into contact with some of the brightest intellectuals and creative people of her day: Sherwood Anderson, E. E. Cummings, John Dos Passos, Alfred A. Knopf, Lewis Mumford—all of whom were sponsors of the Society, and assembled to view such rarely screened productions as *L'Age d'Or* by Luis Buñuel and classics such as Pudovkin's *Mother*, Eisenstein's *Potemkin*, and Stroheim's *Greed*. Bourke-White was exposing herself to the best in creative cinema and surely developed an awareness of the kinds of films that might be historically important. Unfortunately, that awareness ceased to extend over her own films. Bourke-White completely lost her passion for cinema over the next few years.

Throughout the latter part of 1933 the United States economy was improving and Bourke-White's business was picking up, but not fast enough. She faced an almost constant shortage of cash in 1933, which put her in the unenviable position of having to evade bill collectors at her door and borrow money from a friend to help make ends meet. Her situation was so bad that on October 30, 1933, Bourke-White asked her mother to pay the next premium on her New York Life Insurance policy. She had just begun a new project: "I'm doing the rotunda for NBC, and it's a swell job. It would be great fun if I didn't have to work under such pressure. . . . It is such a shame because it is one thing I should give quite a lot of thought to. However, I'm getting grand publicity and all that and I'm happy to do the work."

At the initial stage of the mural project for NBC's new studios in Rockefeller Center, New York City, Bourke-White had no reason to be anything but happy about doing the work. The intense pressure of getting a massive job done fast exhilarated her. There were even some serious dangers associated with taking the pictures, which she met with her usual verve.

The mural was supposed to represent radio, with various panels showing microphones, sending tubes, loudspeakers, generators, antennae towers, and other devices. To get some of the pictures

NBC mural, Rockefeller Center, New York City, 1934.

Bourke-White had to work between midnight and 6:00 a.m., when the transmitting equipment was turned off, in order to avoid possible electrocution. Only during those midnight hours would the engineers allow her behind the heavy glass walls that protected the electronic apparatus she wanted to photograph.

"At dawn the time would come when they had to warm up the tubes to begin broadcasting. Always I had one more picture that I wanted to take. They would say 'Move over or you will be electrocuted,' and I would pick out something closer to the door. At last they would grab my camera and say 'You must get out of here or you will be electrocuted.' They would shut me out, close the heavy door and broadcasting would begin."

That type of drama in her life helped cultivate her particular allure. But there was another drama associated with the mural's execution that Bourke-White never told publicly.

To begin with, Bourke-White had a great deal of difficulty with the NBC executives in charge of approving the design of the mural. Her first few proposals were rejected, and at the last minute a series of exasperating meetings were held to try to come up with a design everyone concerned could live with. Gradually, Bourke-White became convinced that the instigator of the difficulties was Drix Duryea, the photographer who had been commissioned to make the mural-size enlargements from her negatives.

Apparently, on Friday, November 10, twenty-four hours before the mural was supposed to open to the public, Duryea went into the chief engineer's office with a four-page letter listing all the difficulties he claimed he had had with Bourke-White. He complained that the negatives she had delivered did not cover the pictures in the layout, and that he could not get the enlargements done in time for the opening unless he could retake the necessary photographs himself. The engineer gave Duryea permission to rephotograph the things Bourke-White had already done. The opening of the mural was delayed, and Duryea replaced a number of Bourke-White's photographs with his own and received major credit for the whole setup. Bourke-White was not even invited to the opening of the mural.

The situation was not finally resolved until the end of January, when Bourke-White's lawyer and friend Frank Altschul intervened on her behalf. NBC agreed to pay Bourke-White $3,500, give her rights to her negatives, and credit Drix Duryea solely for the execution of the mural. A great deal of publicity for Bourke-White had been lost because the thousands of people who filed by the mural just after the opening saw no mention of her name beside it. That was later corrected, however. Bourke-White also got complete credit for the mural project when *Architectural Record* magazine reviewed it in their August 1934 issue.

The circumstances surrounding her work on the NBC mural had been devastating, nonetheless the project aroused Bourke-White's enthusiasm for what she saw as a fascinating new use for photography.

She felt that photo-murals had applications not only for public buildings like Radio City Music Hall, but also in the home or business office.

Bourke-White made many murals besides the one for NBC. She made one for the Aluminum Company of America, which was hung in the Ford pavilion at the Chicago World's Fair in 1934, and others for the Amoskeag Textile Corporation, Cannon Towels, and Lehigh Portland Cement Company. Bourke-White also made a mural of Magnitogorsk for the Soviet Embassy in New York, and *The New York Times* of June 24, 1934, ran a picture of Bourke-White standing in front of it with the consul of the USSR, Leonid M. Tolokonski.

Although in 1933 Bourke-White entered into experiments with cinema and photo-murals, in 1934 she concentrated her activities for the most part in areas of work in which she already had an established interest. She strengthened her involvement with matters pertaining to the Soviet Union, for instance, by becoming a member of the Friends of the Soviet Union. An exhibition of her Russian photographs was shown at the first convention of the Friends in New York early in 1934. Later that year she agreed to let the Friends use her name on the sponsoring committee for a series of monthly dinners.

In the spring of 1934 Bourke-White also became a member of the Film and Photo League. In April she had sponsored the first annual motion picture and costume ball presented by the League. Other sponsors included Erskine Caldwell, Ralph Steiner, Berenice Abbott, Reginald Marsh, Lee Strasberg, George Gershwin, Burgess Meredith, and James Cagney, among others. Following the ball, Tom Brandon, one of the League's officers, invited her to endorse the League itself, advising her in his letter that endorsing the League meant endorsing their program, which he summarized as follows: "1. To develop the art of still and movie photography. 2. To make and spread workers' films, to popularize Soviet films. 3. To expose and counteract pro-war and pro-fascist films." Bourke-White agreed.

Her interest in socialism and in things Soviet provoked her to subscribe to the *Daily Worker* in 1934 and 1935, and in late spring 1934 Bourke-White's last major project involving her Russian photographs, "Margaret Bourke-White's *U.S.S.R. Photographs*," was published.

This was a portfolio consisting of twenty-four gravure reproductions, each 9⅛ inches x 13 inches printed on special "antique tone" paper measuring 14 inches x 20 inches. The edition, which was brought out by the Argus Company, was limited to one thousand copies, each autographed by Bourke-White herself. Each copy sold for $15.00, and within two years most had been purchased.

In her introduction to the portfolio, Bourke-White wrote:

» Three trips to the Soviet Union taught me it is more than a land of windswept steppes, villages gathered into collective farms, rising factories and growing power dams. Behind the machines stand men and women. They transform the economic life of their country which in turn transforms them. Blast furnaces look the same in Magnitogorsk as in Essen or Pittsburgh. What makes Soviet Russia the new land of the machine are the new social relations of the men and women around the machine. The new man—young shock brigadier on construction or bearded peasant coming from farm to factory—and with him, on an equal footing, the new woman operating drill presses, studying medicine and engineering, are integral parts of a people working collectively toward a common goal. . . . In selecting the photographs for this portfolio from the hundreds I have taken, I chose those which show these men and women rather than their machines. Soviet Russia's story is not only one of the building of industry; it is the story of a people progressing steadily toward richer living. . . . «

Her expression of support for the Soviet system did not extend to any rallying on her part for socialism in America. Collective labor had its place in Russia, but as far as Bourke-White was concerned, independent labor was the only method by which she prospered; and in 1934, prosper she did.

Her solicitation for business the previous spring, coupled with fairer economic winds, helped to increase Bourke-White's gross income to over $35,000. Financially speaking, 1934 was the Bourke-White studio's most successful year. It was the year in which Bourke-White began to do a great deal of highly lucrative work (in black-and-white and color) for the food pages of the *Saturday Evening Post*, *Vanity Fair*, *The Delineator*, and other popular magazines. To accommodate the increased workload she moved her studio and her staff of eight to larger quarters at 521 Fifth Avenue in Manhattan.

In 1934 Bourke-White was working both in color and black-and-white. She charged double her black-and-white rates for color photographs, and for good reason. A color photo in an advertisement was a very rare sight in 1934 magazines, and therefore delivered a great deal more impact than one in conventional black-and-white. Advertisers understood they had to pay more for the extra impact of color. That is still true for the most part today, but in 1934 making a color photograph was a long and frustrating technical ordeal. The process she used required three exposures, using three separate filters on three separate glass plates, each of which had to be painstakingly photoengraved for printing in a magazine.

There was only one engraver in New York licensed to manufacture the plates, and Bourke-White had constant fights with him over faulty registration of the negatives, underexposure, and generally bad service. Remarkably, Bourke-White managed to prevail over those problems and developed quite a reputation for her color work, even to the point of being recognized as something of an authority on the subject.

Bourke-White ceased using color when she gave up advertising photography in 1935, and did not return to work seriously with color until the 1950s, when she did a series of color photographs portraying several regions of the United States from the air for *Life* magazine.

Aviation photography was an endeavor that Bourke-White first took up in 1934, when Pan Am hired her to photograph their new terminal in Miami. They wanted her to do "the story of aviation," everything from loading passengers' luggage to the navigation equipment in the cockpit, and there was a possibility for a mural. TWA hired Bourke-White later that year to do a similar job for them, and in the fall of 1935 Eastern Airlines contracted Bourke-White's services for photographs of the cities of their routes from the air. Those jobs were the beginning of Bourke-White's strong attachment to flying—a passion really—which led to many aviation-related assignments over the following two decades.

During this period magazine advertisements were the main outlet for Bourke-White's photographs, but her pictures also continued to reach the museum audience. In May 1934 five of her photographs were accepted for the third Detroit salon of pictorial photography. The group comprised pictures of radio-receiving tubes, storage tanks for gas, a man working on organ pipes, Stalin's mother, a boat towing logs. Then in November the Cleveland Museum of Art informed her that they were having an exhibition of the work of eight photographic artists, including Steichen, Sheeler, Steiner, and Weston, and they invited Bourke-White to submit ten of her photographs. The exhibition ran for the month of December, and Bourke-White lectured at the Museum on December 14.

Advertising photography kept Bourke-White occupied almost constantly during the spring of 1934, but the work was becoming less and less satisfying: "I was doing a lot of it as one must to support a fancy studio," Bourke-White wrote in an early draft of her autobiography. "It was good technical training as you have to make a rubber tire look like rubber. Otherwise ridiculous, as with the Goodyear 'Margin of Safety' ads in which a little girl on roller skates has fallen in the road and the onrushing car stops miraculously two feet before striking her because of the Goodyear 'Margin of Safety,' which is chalked in white across the street."

Although necessity dictated that she stick with advertising photography for the moment, Bourke-White's instinctive desire to convey something of the meaning of the times in which she lived drew her increasingly toward news photography. It was only a matter of two years before *Life* magazine would give birth to the art of the photo-essay. But *Life* was not the first American publication to demonstrate the vast communicative power in collections of photographs that portrayed current events. One of the forerunners of the *Life* concept was Max L. Schuster's *Eyes on the World*, published by Simon and Schuster in 1935.

In March 1934, knowing of Bourke-White's interest in pictorial publishing, Schuster invited her to take part in the project. The publisher explained that his plans were flexible enough to include an annual book of pictorial history as well as a more frequent periodical publication. It was still too early for him to know whether the intended magazine would be a quarterly, monthly, biweekly, or weekly, but he definitely hoped to supplement the proposed yearbook with a magazine, provided he could obtain the type of pictures he wanted quickly enough and in sufficient quantity to justify more frequent publication. Schuster knew that his magazine proposal would require establishing firsthand contact with the most creative photographers and strategic newspicture sources in all the important cities of the world. Perhaps because the magazine project proved to be so incredibly unwieldy, or because Simon and Schuster learned that Henry Luce had been working on the same idea for months and had already laid the groundwork for his new magazine, only one *Eyes on the World*, based on the world events of 1934, was ever published.

When Schuster's book was published, in the spring of 1935, Bourke-White herself reviewed it for *The Nation*:

» E*yes on the World* represents a new method of communication. We have had books of pictures before, we have weeklies which digest the news, we have rotos and newsreels which are sketchy and uncoordinated, but *Eyes on the World* gives us a vivid picture of the year as a whole, classified and edited. It is true that many people may quarrel with Mr. Schuster's editing, but none is apt to deny that this is a vivid and stimulating way to delineate a year. We have strikers dying in Toledo, violence on the coast, the jobless sleeping on the sidewalks, cows being shot in the drought-stricken cornbelt, the story of America's year told in headlines and photographs that are full of conflict and bloodshed. . . . We all of us remember having read about these things in the daily press. We even will remember many of the pictures reproduced here. But *Eyes on the World* does something to these memories of ours. It condenses them in a form that is startling and vivid. «

One of the domestic disaster areas Bourke-White mentions in the review of *Eyes on the World*—"the drought-stricken cornbelt"—was the focus of an assignment she herself had carried out for *Fortune* in August 1934. The drought ran from the Dakotas to the Texas panhandle. It was such an extensive area to cover that she chartered a plane, a primitive Curtiss Robin. She had to complete the story in five days in order to meet the magazine's October issue deadline.

Barnstorming with her camera through five states, Bourke-White saw from the air a landscape totally devastated from lack of moisture. But much more than the land, the plight of the farmers and their families left a deep and lasting impression on her. "I had never seen people caught helpless like this in total tragedy," she wrote in *Portrait of Myself*. "They had no defense. . . . Here were faces engraved with the very paralysis of despair. These were faces I could not pass by."

After photographing the drought, it was very hard indeed for Bourke-White to return to advertising. "The drought had been a powerful eye-opener and had shown me that right here in my own country there were worlds about which I knew almost nothing." The urge to show those new worlds to others was already strong in her, and growing strong was her conviction that her photographs should have social significance. If other Americans saw the suffering that the nation's farmers were enduring in the cornbelt, she reasoned, would this not be enough to stimulate some form of drought relief? Bourke-White knew that photographs had the power to influence people's thinking. She knew people believed the stories pictures told. In her advertising work she had directed the power in her photographs toward the goal of building a consumer's faith in a product so that the consumer would feel confident about going out and buying whatever product he or she had seen in the ad. The process usually amounted to puffing the product up far beyond realistic expectations, or in other words, falsifying and distorting facts.

Ultimately, Bourke-White decided to leave advertising because she could no longer endure doing work in which facts were falsified and distorted. She wanted to awaken others to new worlds as she herself had been awakened earlier in Russia, and earlier still, as she had been awakened to the drama of industry.

During the fall of 1934 Bourke-White increasingly sought avenues through which to channel her interest in news and socially significant photography. One avenue she investigated further was the Film and Photo League. Since the spring her name had been on the League's letterhead but she had been far too busy to participate in their activities. Bourke-White generally followed the same pattern with other organizations she sponsored, lending her prestigious name and contributing a few dollars but not participating actively because of her busy work schedule.

Then in December Bourke-White wrote to the League's director, Albert Carroll, in reply to his request that she lecture to the group's membership. She apologized that she would be too busy to commit herself to a lecture engagement, but asked Carroll to fill her in on what the League had been trying to accomplish.

December 1934 also marks the beginning of Bourke-White's association with the NEA news syndicate. NEA circulated a broadside two days before the end of the year proclaiming the start of Margaret Bourke-White's "Pictorial Parade from Washington." She covered Washington, D.C., for NEA exclusively for a few months in 1935.

One curious anecdote that survived from her Washington assignment for NEA was related in a May 1935 radio interview. The interviewer asked Bourke-White if she had ever been scared of an assignment. She was never scared, exactly, Bourke-White replied, but she had to admit she was pretty nervous and jittery about a picture she had taken of President Roosevelt: "It was all on account of a dream," Bourke-White said.

» It was one of those rush by plane pictures for a news agency. And I had my appointments for the next morning. That night I dreamed that I broke my camera, dropping the bulbs like a clumsy fool every time I set up my equipment. When I went for my appointment to the White House the next morning, I was in a panic. But everything went smooth as cream. The President was charming, and posed with no mishap to my machinery. But here's the joke. On the White House lawn as I was set up for an exterior my arm hit the camera. The tripod collapsed and the camera broke into a thousand pieces. «

Immediately following her Washington assignment, Bourke-White started working for TWA, then known as Transcontinental and Western Airlines. The photographic survey she put together for TWA took in practically every operation of the airline and while she traveled to points west she was able to continue doing work for one of her advertising clients, taking pictures of dozens of brave and virile pilots smoking Chesterfields.

Since TWA's routes covered the western and southwestern United States, Bourke-White also managed to fit in some additional work on the Dust Bowl in Texas for NEA. Caption material for a large set of those 1935 drought negatives reveals just how shocking conditions seemed to Bourke-White out west that year:

» Skeleton of a horse— died—no water . . . Oval-shaped barn—tenants are going in for these round barns as an experiment because the wind can't tear them up . . . Cattle near Dalhart showing decrepit pens. In normal times this would never happen. Farmers would keep their places up—now too poor. Note scrubby condition of cattle. This comes from underfeeding. . . . Family packed up in truck and moving to another state. Was awfully lucky to get this. The farmer was lucky to have his truck left after he sold out. He managed to save his truck and is leaving drought-stricken country for good. Will go anywhere where he can get work. Usually go south into cotton country. Cotton farmers hire help. The things on this truck are all they possess. The hail storm came up just after I took this and hail beat down on their household things. . . . Woman at mail box on wheel. Her husband had been working in wheat. Now on relief-road job. Probably gets a little over $2.00 a day or $8.00 a week, but is allowed only 9 days a month. Based on size of family—he has two children. A man with five gets 13 days a month. . . . Mother of children in bed—apologized . . . Canadian River Bed—largest river in North Texas—dried up from drought. Hardly a trickle of water in bottom. Very little good to cattle. «

———

The remainder of 1935 was taken up with airlines photography. TWA sent Bourke-White all the way to California that spring, where she took the opportunity to visit her contacts in Hollywood and met, among others, cinematographer James Wong Howe, who was an admirer of Bourke-White's work. Later in the year, Howe sent Bourke-White a few pictures of herself, taken while she was visiting MGM's studios. In return he asked that she please send him an autograph.

While she was on the coast, the photographer Martin Munkacsi wrote to thank Bourke-White for a photograph she had sent him (of limestone saws in Indiana) and hoped that the photograph was only her messenger and that she would follow it shortly to pay him a visit in New York.

Bourke-White returned to New York when the TWA job was finished at the end of April 1935, and in early May discussed her adventures in a radio interview program sponsored by *Mademoiselle* magazine. The interviewer was Henriette Harrison, radio director of the YMCA.

» *Mrs. Harrison:* To tell you the truth, I feel quite proud of today's capture. For I've brought down with my little celebrity gun Margaret Bourke-White, the famous industrial photographer, who was recently included in the list of the twenty most able business women of the country. And when I say brought down I mean it literally. For

Miss Bourke-White has crawled through miles of Russian coal mines on her stomach to get a picture, teetered so close to molten steel that the varnish on her camera was blistered off, has been living in the clouds for the past month. Isn't that so my dear?

Bourke-White: Well, no, not exactly, it's true that I've been out west shooting pictures from the airplane. But mostly the atmosphere was so clear that there weren't any clouds. But that's an exaggeration. I remember one cloud in particular—a dear little soft fluffy pink cloud, in fact it was the heroine of one of our trips. It was sunrise and we were flying about two miles high over the San Bernardino Mountains. And between us and one dazzling snow-covered peak was this lovely little cloud bathed in the early morning sunlight. I shouted to Jack through the speaking tube to bank and to dip and to stand the plane on its tail so that I could get pictures of the cloud from all possible angles. It was positively the most overworked little cloud west of the Mississippi.

Mrs. Harrison: For goodness sakes, when did you start to work?

Bourke-White: Oh, about 2:30 every morning. I would call up the airport from my hotel or wherever I was staying and the pilots would read me the weather reports. If these sounded good we would start out at once, for we usually traveled about 200 miles to 400 miles to location and it was important to get there by sunrise. You see the morning light is by far the best for picture taking in the air. . . .

Mrs. Harrison: You got caught in the dust storms. Do please tell us all about them. Are they as terrible as they sound?

Bourke-White: They are simply unbelievable. Even when there isn't a real "duster," which is what they are called out there, in progress, there is dust everywhere. You eat dust. It gets through the ice box and into the butter. It creeps into the baby's milk. People shut their windows and doors and stop up cracks with cloths and when they go out they put towels around their mouths or hold wet sponges to their noses. The dust banks up around chicken coops and barns. People never get through digging. We passed whole families on trucks going to other states to look for jobs. The wheat had actually been blown out of the ground in some areas.

Mrs. Harrison: Good Heavens! It sounds terrifying. . . . How did you get your pictures of the dust storm? I saw some in the papers.

Bourke-White: The chief problem was the light.

It gets dark at late twilight during a duster. And the light turns a dark yellow. And then there's the dust—so much of it and so knife-like when it hits that the lenses of my camera were cut to pieces. I had to change them every time I took a picture. «

Bourke-White also put her observations about the suffering the dusters were causing into an article titled "Dust Changes America," which appeared in *The Nation* on May 22, 1935. She wrote:

» As short a time as eight months ago there was an attitude of false optimism. Things will get better, the farmers would say. We're not as hard hit as other states. The government will help out. This can't go on. But this year there is an atmosphere of utter hopelessness. Nothing to do. No use digging out your chicken coops and pigpens after the last duster because the next one will be coming soon. No use trying to keep the house clean. No use fighting off that foreclosure any longer. No use even hoping to give your cattle anything to chew on when their food crops have literally blown out of the ground. «

With the appearance of the article in *The Nation,* Bourke-White moved herself into the growing circle of artists of that period who became keen observers and vocal critics of American social conditions. *You Have Seen Their Faces,* the forerunner of such classic social documentary books as *Let Us Now Praise Famous Men,* was the project that emerged from Bourke-White's interest in focusing attention on the plight of the American farmer. While preparations for *You Have Seen Their Faces* were under way, Bourke-White also became involved in the First American Artists Congress, an effort aimed at protesting the spread of reactionary trends in the United States. The "Call" to the Congress cited a "constant attack against freedom of expression" in the United States which was undermining the freedom of artists.

On August 5, 1935, Stuart Davis, the Secretary of the Congress, sent Bourke-White a copy of the "Call" and asked her to put her name on the list of supporters. Bourke-White was in Detroit, on a job for Buick, but answered upon her return on August 16: "I am very much in sympathy with your plan of the Call and I am entirely willing to sign. . . . This is a subject in which I am most interested and you can count on my positive support."

Davis wrote her again on August 23, enclosing a report he hoped would give Bourke-White a general idea of the organizing committee's preliminary efforts. It had been suggested, he said, that Bourke-White prepare a paper on the artist in the Soviet Union, and Davis hoped she would be able to cooperate since her familiarity with the situation at first hand gave her unique qualifications for a talk on that subject.

She was unable to respond to Davis's request until early January 1936, about a month before the Congress was scheduled to convene in New York. She wrote: "I am most willing to deliver the paper on the Soviet Union, if you wish. I cannot help but feel however that it would be more convincing if it came from someone who has been there more recently than I have. But if the committee has decided that I should be the one to do it I shall consent."

Bourke-White's professional work prevented her from actively participating in the planning of the Congress. But she did invite Ralph Steiner, Paul Strand, Alfred Stieglitz, Anton Bruehl, and Edward Steichen. In a letter to each of them, dated November 7, 1935, Bourke-White explained: "The aim of the Congress is to discuss the critical situation that has arisen with the approach of War and Fascism as a threat to culture. Those of us who have signed the Call for this Congress did so in the belief that such reactionary tendencies as have appeared in the form of censorship and destruction of works of art, and in the suppression of civil liberties, are symptomatic of more serious conditions to come. *It can happen here,* but the artists can organize and help to stop it."

Steiner and Strand both signed the "Call," as did Berenice Abbott, Ben Shahn, and about four hundred other prominent artists. Strand wrote to Bourke-White saying: "As to the aim of the Congress you are completely right as to my allegiance." Strand went on in the letter to say how pleased he was to hear from Ralph Steiner that Bourke-White had gotten something from the photographs in his Mexican Portfolio, which Steiner had recently shown her. "Possibly they explain why I did not attempt to do anything in the Soviet Union in a limited time," Strand continued. "And here is America still waiting to be really photographed, a challenge to all of us, to the painters as well."

Bourke-White also invited Edward Weston to sign the "Call," but Weston's opinion of the Congress was precisely the opposite of Strand's. Weston wrote to Bourke-White on February 6, 1936, one week before the Congress opened: "If the Congress of A.A. was not so one-sided in its 'againsts,' I would be more interested. It should include communism, capitalism, prohibition, amongst many other contemporary manifestations of greed, fear, and will to power. True, that it can happen here—even communism. Thanks for your kind letter. If you are ever in this part of the world, will be glad to welcome you. Cordially, Edward Weston."

Bourke-White's commitment to be present for the Artists Congress in February forced her to break briefly from her work for Eastern Airlines. The Eastern job had commenced in October 1935, when Bourke-White had signed an elaborate contract. She even had to get special permission to do independent advertising work in the cities to which Eastern would be flying her for the job. That permission was granted after some fuss, and she then sent out letters to several advertising agencies and public relations departments of major companies soliciting business en route. She was scheduled to fly to Philadelphia, Washington, D.C., Winston-Salem, Charleston, Jackson, Nashville, Chicago, Baltimore, Richmond, Atlanta, Miami, New Orleans, and Indianapolis.

The Eastern job was completed in the early spring of 1936, which freed the remainder of the year for more varied adventures. Bourke-White herself called 1936 a year "unlike any year I have ever lived through," and attributed the unusual variety of exciting new endeavors she began that year to having made a "definite choice" about the direction of her career. That definite choice, she believed, put her on the right path, allowing her to be receptive to "the best of everything that came."

The choice to which she refers was her final decision to exit from advertising photography, a move that was ultimately precipitated by a curious dream, which she recalled in *Portrait of Myself:*

» I still remember the mood of terror. Great unfriendly shapes were rushing toward me, threatening to crush me down. As they drew closer, I recognized them as the Buick cars I had been photographing. They were moving toward me in a menacing zigzag course, their giant hoods raised in jagged alarming shapes as though determined to swallow me. Run as fast as I could, I could not escape them. As they moved faster, I began to stumble, and as they towered over me, pushing me down, I woke up to find that I had fallen out of bed and was writhing on the floor with my back strained. I decided that if a mere dream could do this to me, the time had come to get out of this type of photography altogether. If I believed in piloting one's own life, then I should go ahead and pilot mine. Since photography was a craft I respected, let me treat it with respect. «

Bourke-White made a resolution that from then on, for the rest of her life, she would undertake only those photographic assignments she felt could be done in a "creative and constructive way." After 1936 advertising was excluded entirely. Above all, she was seeking a personal way of responding to the emergent trend toward socially significant expression in the arts.

By coincidence, Bourke-White heard that Erskine Caldwell, author of *Tobacco Road,* then a best-selling novel and successful Broadway play, was interested in collaborating with the photographer on a book that would prove that the world of *Tobacco Road,* a world modeled on the poverty and racism of the United States South, was authentic, and not exaggerated fiction, as many of Caldwell's critics claimed. Literary agent Maxim Lieber relayed Bourke-White's interest in working with Caldwell on the project, and by January 1936 the novelist agreed in principle to work with Bourke-White.

Bourke-White wrote to Caldwell on March 9, "This is just to tell you that I am happier about the book I am to do with you than anything I have had a chance to work on for the last two years. I have felt keenly for some time that I was turning my camera too often to advertising subjects and too little in the direction of something that might have some social significance. I am happier about this than I can say. If I had a chance to choose from every living writer in America, I would choose you first as the person I would like to do such a book with. And to have you drop out of a clear sky just when I have decided that I wanted to take pictures that are closer to life seems too good to be true. Mr. Lieber has told you, I believe, that I will be ready toward the middle or end of June. It probably will be closer to the end of the month or really July if that is satisfactory to you. And again, I am looking forward to it so much."

She accompanied her letter with a photograph, meant as a gift, not knowing that it would be the first example of her work Caldwell had seen that was not a magazine reproduction. Caldwell was grateful for the gift, and upon seeing her work in the original was more than ever impressed with her style.

In the middle of those discussions for the project, which became *You Have Seen Their Faces,* the First Artists Congress opened in New York. Also in February *The Nation* published an important article by Bourke-White, in which she discussed the shift that had occurred in her thinking with respect to photography.

» When the grandeur of industry appeals alike to manufacturer and photographer, the industrial artist is creative and free. The artist's livelihood becomes involved at this point. He likes to think of himself as apart from business. Yet he stands or falls with the business cycle. In a period of prosperity the artist is given the opportunity to develop his technique. He can experiment, learn, grow—and the businessman will help him. But in time of crisis the businessman is too preoccupied or too poor. And even under the best conditions the environment may be antagonistic to the artist. The adoption of the ideals of his customer or patron may require that he abandon his own artistic and social conceptions. How will he escape from this dilemma? Either he adopts those ideals and prospers temporarily, or he repudiates them and becomes increasingly unhappy. At a moment of crisis, he has neither happiness nor prosperity. Like the painter, the photographer is seeking a wider world, one in which the desire for self-realization is not achieved at the cost of his integrity. «

After citing the First Artists Congress as a forum that would confront issues of aesthetic, economic, and social concern to artists, Bourke-White affirms her own position on the matter. "It is my own conviction that defense of their economic needs, as well as their liberty of artistic expression, will inevitably draw artists closer to the struggle of the great masses of American people for security and the abundant life."

In her paper entitled "An Artist's Experience in the Soviet Union," which Bourke-White presented to the Congress, she holds up the Communist state as an exemplary society. Her claims would provoke laughter today, but Bourke-White was applauded when she said:

» National arts are flourishing. The party and government lay down no method or technique, no laws of aesthetics. All types of art are found—abstract, cubist, surrealist. Every artistic experiment that individual artists wish to carry out they can. People in general have the notion that there is an art line laid down by the government, but this is not true. This freedom to experiment—and the opportunity to experiment without worrying about the rent and the grocery bill—points up, more sharply than anything else I can think of, the tremendous difference between the opportunities of the artist under a system like that in the Soviet Union and the situation here. Despite difficulties due to limited availability of equipment and materials, all kinds of creative work go forward. There must be some reason. The excellence of this work is no accident. There is something that happens to the minds of these men because they have found freedom to think. «

Bourke-White did not realize until she returned to Russia in the summer of 1941 how much had changed in the interim, how far off base her remarks at the Artists Congress had really been. Her position on the Russians may not have seemed unusual in 1936. Stalin had only recently begun the mass purges of his enemies, and the truth was not widely known.

Following the Artists Congress, in the spring of 1936, Bourke-White took a two-month trip to Brazil to photograph the growing and manufacturing of coffee for American Can. The trip was also something of a luxury working-vacation for her because she received lavish hospitality from the owners of the coffee plantations, at whose estates she lived for the duration of the trip.

Just prior to flying off to Brazil, Bourke-White signed an agreement with NEA/Acme news services, giving them rights to photographs she would do for them on exclusive assignments.

Since she was in Brazil for April and May and returned to the United States to begin working with Erskine Caldwell on *You Have Seen Their Faces,* which took most of the summer, and then had to deal with the first issue of *Life* magazine in the fall, Bourke-

White did very few assignments for NEA/Acme. Her contract was terminated, in any case, because the director of NEA discovered that Bourke-White had taken photographs of Earl Browder and James W. Ford, the two Communist party candidates for president and vice-president in 1936, which Bourke-White gave to the party to distribute and publish as they saw fit, for free. The photographs were technically the exclusive property of NEA because the news service had assigned Bourke-White to photograph all the candidates for president that year.

So much else was going on in her life that the demise of Bourke-White's relationship with NEA was not a major blow, by any means. She was about to begin work on two of the most important photography projects of her life: *Life* magazine and *You Have Seen Their Faces*. The summer of 1936 was special for another reason as well. Bourke-White and Erskine Caldwell fell in love.

When Bourke-White flew to Georgia in mid-June to begin working with Caldwell, the two met for the first time. Bourke-White's first impression of the novelist was that he was a "very silent, almost inarticulate man," and during the first five days of their work together Bourke-White had to guess what was on his mind. Nonetheless, Bourke-White felt confident because her father had been a quiet type of man also. "I thought I knew how to deal with silent men," she said in an early draft of *Portrait of Myself.*

But on the fifth day Caldwell told her he felt they weren't getting anything accomplished. He felt like a tourist guide, he said, and thought they should give up the whole project. "I was thunderstruck," Bourke-White said. "I had thought we were getting along so well. How could I have been so obtuse as not to even guess things were so far off the track? Of course I cried. And suddenly something very unexpected happened. We fell in love, and beginning with the sixth day, everything worked out fine."

Bourke-White learned a great deal from Caldwell's way of working, which she called "a very quiet, completely receptive approach." While Caldwell was at ease in the South, and capable of relating to people in every region they entered, Bourke-White was unmistakably a Yankee—a foreigner—and she recalled often acting like one. On one occasion when they went into a little cabin to photograph the black woman who lived there, Bourke-White decided to take a picture of her combing her hair, and rearranged everything on her dresser for the sake of superior composition. When they were finished, Caldwell spoke to Bourke-White about what she had done. He pointed out to her that the black woman must have valued her possessions and had tidily arranged them *her* way, which was not the Bourke-White way. This was a new point of view to Bourke-White and she realized she had been callous.

Bourke-White and Caldwell traveled for two months together in the summer of 1936, gathering material for the book in the so-called black belt, the heart of the South, where the most sharecropping and tenant farming were found. That was in Georgia and the region bordering the Mississippi River. They later decided that they had not gathered enough material and returned, in the spring of 1937, to cover the fringes of the areas they had worked in the first time.

In an article for the *Journal-American,* Bourke-White observed that the South they covered for the book "may not be the South of song and story, but it is the South that you bring back on sheets of Panchromatic film. Most of the people we photographed were way too ignorant to know what it was all about. Occasionally we found an interesting condition—a mother who didn't want people to see how poor things were—had lived in better houses and was ashamed. In many cases people did not have the least vestige of pride. In some cases they felt that it was a good thing to take their pictures—to show the world just how bad things were. But usually we encountered plain apathy. . . ."

"People don't realize how serious conditions in this country are," Bourke-White wrote in a letter to one of her former college professors. "We are only hoping that the book may do some good."

Although the complicated issues involved in the sharecropper problem and the labors of her collaboration with Caldwell were enough to preoccupy Bourke-White's mind in the summer of 1936, a comment she made in a radio interview on August 31 reveals yet another dimension of her thinking at this time. The interviewer asked whether there was one picture Bourke-White wanted to take more than any other in the world. Bourke-White replied: "I'd like to photograph the next war, if there's got to be one. I want to start with the starving children and war-widowed women back home. The sinking ships at sea. Guns behind the lines, battles in trenches, and in the sky, and after it is over I want to photograph the desolation war has left. That sequence put right down in black and white may make folks see just how horrible war is and perhaps then I shall have done my little bit toward ending wars for all time."

Only five days after declaring her wish to photograph the next war, Bourke-White took the first step toward making that wish come true. She became one of the first staff photographers for *Life*, signing a contract that bound her to work exclusively for Time Inc. as of October 1, at a salary of $12,000 a year, which included two months' leave each year with pay. She closed her studio at 521 Fifth Avenue and arranged for her staff to be hired by the new magazine as well.

Bourke-White's first assignment was to photograph the enormous chain of dams in the Columbia River basin, a major project of Roosevelt's New Deal. The story was the brainchild of Henry Luce himself, who told Bourke-White to look out for something on a grand scale that might make a cover.

Bourke-White found something for the cover, of course. Her photograph of the Fort Peck Dam became *Life*'s first cover. She also photographed a great deal more in the Northwest than anyone had imagined was out there. "What the Editors expected were construction pictures as only Bourke-White can take them," said the caption introducing her famous Fort Peck Dam essay in *Life*'s first issue. "What the Editors got was a human document of American frontier life which, to them at least, was a revelation."

When the first issue of *Life* came out on November 11, 1936, the magazine itself was a revelation, and quickly became one of the outstanding publishing successes in American history.

As far as Bourke-White was concerned, the *Life* enterprise Luce was tooling up seemed precisely geared to her current photographic aims. There were problems, of course. The editors, for instance, had to be convinced to give photographers credit on the pages where their photographs appeared. A compromise was eventually worked out whereby the editors agreed to credit photographers with their photos when they were used in layouts of four pages or more. Otherwise all credits would appear in a box in a discreet location in the magazine.

Life's editors had the final say about most things pertaining to the pictures they published. That was the nature of the enterprise. The magazine was larger by far than any individual photographer whose work ever appeared in its pages, and an individual photographer generally sacrificed many of his own wishes in return for having his pictures seen in *Life* by millions. Often the particular sensibility a photographer had brought to a picture assignment was completely distorted by the editors, and on occasion such attitudes were the subject of bitter fights between the magazine and photographers such as W. Eugene Smith, who always demanded the right to produce his own layouts.

Bourke-White learned the score with her first story for *Life*. In a memo about the Fort Peck photographs, Bourke-White's secretary wrote: "They grabbed that Fort Peck stuff print by print as it came out of the darkroom, allowing no selection or consideration at all on our part."

Long experience with art directors had made Bourke-White somewhat compliant when it came to layouts. In general, she was sincerely delighted to be part of a brand-new magazine, as she had been when *Fortune* was first published in 1930.

"I must tell you something about my work with the magazine," Bourke-White wrote to a friend in March 1937.

» The idea of it is to present the news of the world in pictures. It is the kind of work I most enjoy doing. There were terrifying floods in the Ohio River Valley last month and I went to Louisville to photograph a city deep in water and lacking any of its usual facilities. Early in the fall I went west to Montana, Washington, and Oregon to photograph huge dams that were being built by the Government. Another time I was in Buffalo taking pictures of the making of parachutes. And so it goes with one thing after another. I'm hardly back in New York before a new assignment takes me away again. «

Microphones, 1934.

Margaret Bourke-White with a mural photograph of an experimental television ''eye,'' 1934.

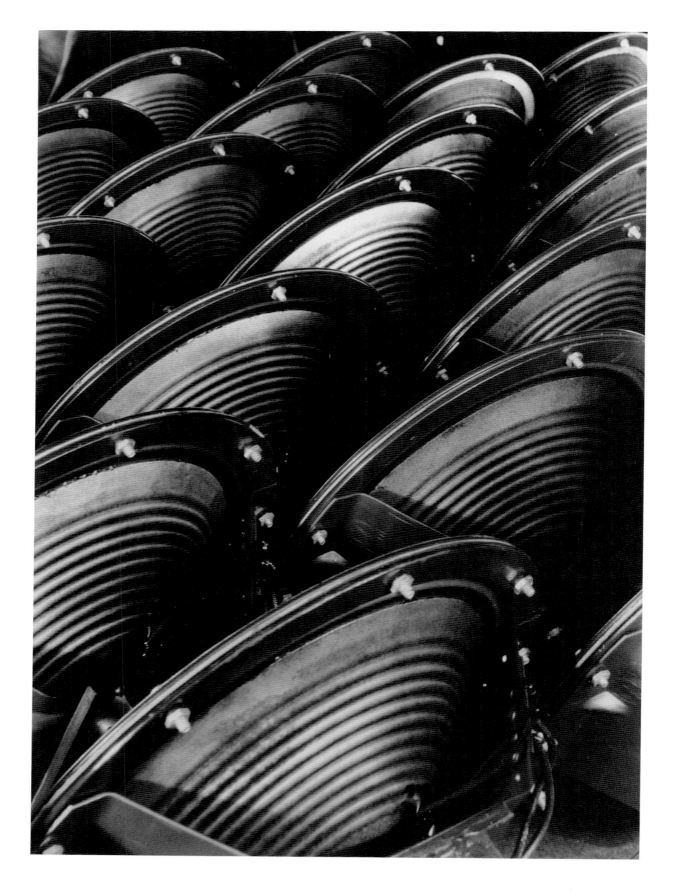

Radio loudspeakers, 1934.

Airplane wings, 1934.

Igor Sikorsky with a plane he designed for Pan American Airways, 1934.

Detail of a TWA plane, 1934.

DC-3 over Manhattan, 1934.

Biplane, about 1934.

"You gave us beer, now give us water." Dust Bowl, 1935.

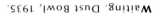

Waiting. Dust Bowl, 1935.

Home scenes, Dust Bowl, 1935.

On the road, 1936.

Belmont, Florida, 1936.

Statesboro, Georgia, 1936.

Tobacco farmer, 1936.

Johns, Mississippi, 1936.

Chain gang, Hood's Chapel, Georgia, 1936.

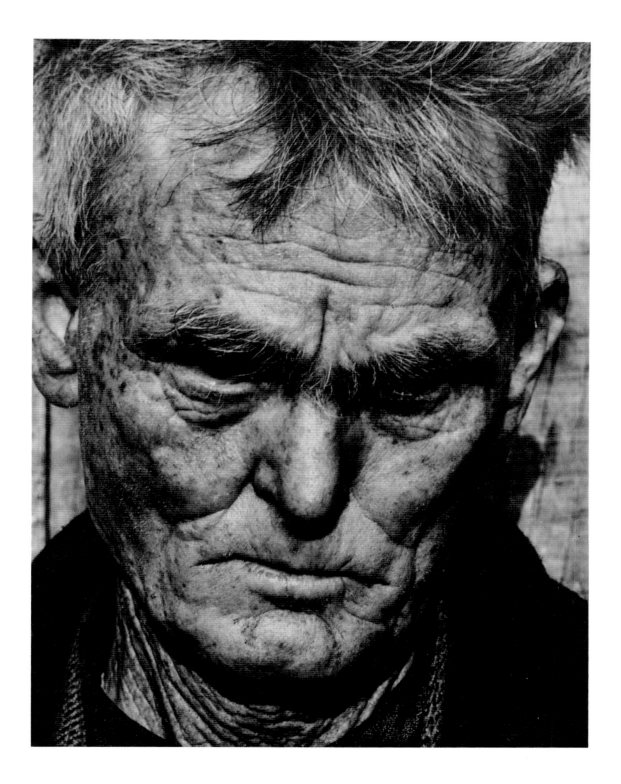

Sharecroppers, 1936.

A number of Margaret Bourke-White's early *Life* assignments were straight news stories; some were straight pictorials; many were Americana features; others were trivia. Few were probing stories of the sort Bourke-White had done on the Fort Peck Dam. But such was the nature of *Life* magazine: the broad borders of its editorial concept encompassed life in all its variety. Practically any story was possible, provided great pictures could be guaranteed.

In particular, *Life* was remarkable for sponsoring the most extraordinary travel excursions for the sake of sending photographers to faraway sites from which no photographs of significance had previously emerged. For instance, *Life* sent Bourke-White to the Arctic Circle in the summer of 1937 for an assignment from which she almost did not return. The pilot of a small plane she had chartered for part of the trip lost his way in a snowstorm and had to make an emergency landing on a small, uncharted inlet. Luckily, the pilot was familiar enough with the area to find his way back to a small village when the storm cleared.

There was always a place in *Life* for exotic or unprecedented phenomena. Bourke-White herself was assigned in 1937 to photograph the use of a new aerosol wetting agent that made ducks sink. For the most part, however, the pages of *Life* were covered with pictures of scenes closer to home. The early *Life* concentrated on the average American: family life, sports, small-town activities.

Among the notable photo-essays on American life published in the salad days of *Life* magazine was Bourke-White's series on Muncie, Indiana, illustrating the daily habits of the town that was the focus of *Middletown,* the landmark sociological study written in the 1920s.

Beaumont Newhall, then curator of photography at the Museum of Modern Art, was sufficiently impressed with her Middletown essay to ask Bourke-White for the loan of one of the pictures from that series for an exhibition of American art that was to be presented at the Musée du Jeu de Paume in Paris. Needless to say, Bourke-White was happy to lend a print for the Paris show. One year earlier, Bourke-White had lent five of her photographs for the Museum of Modern Art's "Photography 1839–1937" exhibition, the show from which Newhall's classic history of photography emerged.

When he first saw the Middletown essay in *Life*, Newhall wrote to Bourke-White to say that "Viewed as a whole," the Middletown series was the "finest piece of documentary photography" it had been his fortune to see. "It is so embracing, so thorough, and so brilliant from a photographic standpoint," Newhall added. He was particularly impressed by Bourke-White's use of synchronized photo-flash. He felt this was much more artfully handled in "Conversation Club" (*Life,* May 10, 1937) than in the average news picture for which the flash gun was generally placed too close to the camera to obtain proper modeling.

Life's photographers frequently were acclaimed for the crafty techniques they initiated in their work for the magazine. But photographic tricks were by no means the key to *Life*'s success. *Life* attributed its immense appeal to the new "picture and word editorial technique" its editors had developed to make "the truth about the world we live in infinitely more exciting, more easily absorbed, more alive than it has ever been made before."

The combining of pictures and words in a brilliant new way was also responsible to a large measure for the success of *You Have Seen Their Faces* when it was published in the fall of 1937. The reviews of the book almost unanimously called attention to the manner in which the book reversed conventional roles for words and pictures. The method of making pictures the body of the text, while the written material served as illustrations, was precisely the method *Life* used. But in *You Have Seen Their Faces* the picture-and-word technique was devoted to bringing to light several aspects of one story—the plight of the sharecropper in the southern United States—not a timely panoply of current events.

Simultaneous with publication of the book in the fall of 1937, *Life* ran a series of Bourke-White *You Have Seen Their Faces* pictures. The *Life* feature had great promotion value for the book, and led to sales that soared far beyond everyone's expectations.

Although sharecropping was an important issue in America, problems of greater magnitude were brewing in the world at large. In March 1938 Germany annexed Austria and was threatening to do the same with the Sudetenland in northern Czechoslovakia.

When *Life* decided to send Bourke-White to

Czechoslovakia to cover the turmoil developing there, she and Caldwell decided to collaborate on a book about the Sudetenland, and they sailed together for a four-month trip to the region on the last day of March that year. The material they collected during their travels in Czechoslovakia formed the basis for *North of the Danube*, published by The Viking Press in 1939.

North of the Danube was less successful than *You Have Seen Their Faces*, in terms of both design and sales. The book is an interesting historical documentary, but it lacks dramatic focus on a particular issue. Partly an astute pictorial display of the beautiful landscapes and exotic peasant life of Czechoslovakia, *North of the Danube* is also an attempt to expose the oppressive tactics the Germans were using to overtake the Sudetenland in defiance of the Treaty of Versailles. Unfortunately, the harmonious blend of pictures and words which worked so beautifully in *You Have Seen Their Faces* was lacking in *North of the Danube*.

Oddly, Bourke-White declined to include notes of her own in the book. The writing is all Caldwell's. But on November 14, 1938, in a lecture Bourke-White delivered to a gathering of the Advertising Women of New York, she fully described her impressions of the tragic conflict she had seen building in Czechoslovakia during her travels there:

» It is not generally realized how full Czechoslovakia was of paid German propaganda agents. They were German citizens, there on German passports, and their job was to make the people feel that, while there was a great deal of unemployment in the Sudeten area, as soon as Germany took the country over, Hitler would see personally that everybody had a job.

Their aim with journalists and photographers like myself was a little more subtle. They started out by entertaining us, showing us around the Prague nightclubs. They began by poking fun at the Czechs and ended up by trying to show us examples of Czech oppression. So I shook Mr. Hitler's entertainment squad, and even evaded Czech government officials, who wanted to be courteous and helpful, because I wanted to travel around the country by myself and form an unbiased opinion of the Czech oppression.

And this is what I found. Everywhere I saw that

Photographing a Canadian logjam, 1937.

the Czech government had built schools for each language minority that lived there. In the Sudeten area there were German language schools; in the North were Polish and Czech language schools side by side; in the South were schools that taught Slovak, and Czech, and Hungarian for the minorities that lived there. In the far eastern part of Ruthenia the government had built Russian-language schools for the peasants who spoke Russian, and these were in primitive parts of the country where there had never been schools before. In Uzhorod (the capital of Ruthenia, which has recently been given to Hungary) the Czech government had even built Hebrew schools where orthodox Jewish boys studied the Talmud.

Pick up any newspaper of this last week and you will be able to guess what is happening to those orthodox Jewish families in the areas which Hitler has "liberated" as he likes to call it. [Nearly 500,000 Czech Jews were murdered by the Nazis between 1938 and 1945.]

With Erskine Caldwell in a London television studio, 1938. BBC photograph.

Everywhere the language of the minority was used along with the Czech language. If you went to the spa at Karlsbad, you drank your mineral water. If you were a Czech, you drank from a mug labeled with the Czech name of Karlovy Vary, or if you were a German, you selected a mug marked Karlsbad. But if you went to Karlsbad today and sipped from a mug marked Karlovy Vary, I believe you would get your mug broken. And you would be lucky if it were only your mug that got broken. **«**

In closing her talk to the Advertising Women, Bourke-White reveals how four months of confronting history in Czechoslovakia had changed her outlook on photography:

» Events in the world are so serious today that it is important to do something about it. Photographers can do a good deal because the truth has a way of creeping into pictures. Perhaps a woman photographer can do a little more than a man because she can slip around better, she can get appointments with people more easily, and if she is showing something behind the news that the people around her don't want shown, perhaps she isn't always thrown out quite so promptly. At any rate, there is so much happening today, so much behind the news that affects our lives, that it is the function of the photographer to show the truth. **«**

Although Bourke-White was personally interested in conveying truths about the world that would otherwise be obscured, such was not generally true of the aims of *Life* magazine. Designed as it was to dazzle its readers, *Life* believed that Americans did not want to be hit over the head with a magazine that uncovered disturbing new facts. They wanted to be startled, perhaps, but by the novelty of things they had never before seen in a magazine, not by political and social questions that would force them to confront the burning issues of the day. *Life*, therefore, could never provide a comprehensive outlet for Bourke-White's creative endeavors. She had to follow independent paths to pursue her broadening interest in the social and political ramifications of world events.

Producing a book such as *North of the Danube*, which attempted to expose the truth about a dangerous political situation, was one path Bourke-White explored. She also extended the list of her sponsorships to include such organizations as the American Youth Congress, the League of Women Shoppers, and the League of American Writers—all groups whose activities, in one form or another, were organized to protest the rise of fascism and political repression. It was not unusual to find Bourke-White at a luncheon for the benefit of sending relief supplies to the antifascists in the Spanish Civil War. That was her way of participating in the struggle to save freedom and democracy.

Amid all her other involvements, and partially against her better judgment, as she explains in *Portrait of Myself,* in February 1939 Bourke-White married Erskine Caldwell. Clearly, Bourke-White could never have been expected to fill the role of housewife as it was then defined. Instead, she saw her new position as that of working wife, and considered the situation a special challenge. She succinctly expressed her views on being married in a 1939 letter to Norman Cousins.

Cousins, then an associate editor of *Current History* magazine, had asked Bourke-White to contribute to an article he was putting together, which was to be entitled "The Married Woman in Business." At that time various states were threatening to limit or curtail the employment of married women in public service and private industry. Cousins's article pointed out the fallacies in the arguments supporting such restrictive legislation and reviewed the question in light of America's democratic tradition.

Also invited to state their views on the subject were Eleanor Roosevelt, Katherine Cornell, Dorothy Thompson, and Helen Keller, among others. Bourke-White wrote:

» Women both married and unmarried have helped to build our country and it would be a retrogression for democracy if any distinction were made between them. In all progressive countries of the world both married and unmarried women work. It is only in reactionary countries that women are denied work because of their marital status.

Surely today, when the forces of reaction are sweeping the world, it is more important than ever before for a democracy like ours to permit the full development of its people. No democracy can afford to arrest the mental development of women by forcing them to give up outside work upon marriage, nor should it deprive itself of the enriching effect of the work performed by its married women. «

The forces of reaction began to swamp Europe in the fall of 1939, at which time practically all other social issues seemed to shrink in importance. *Life* immediately sent Bourke-White to cover the momentous developments overseas, and, as she wrote in a letter to New York Senator Robert F. Wagner shortly before she left, she was very excited about the prospect of witnessing how people functioned during wartime:

» *Life* magazine is sending me to France and England to cover the life of the people under conditions of war. We all feel that while interesting pictures have been arriving, there has been nothing yet to show how people actually live in times like these. It is my job to make that as real as possible, and I am looking forward to the assignment as one of the most important I have ever had. «

While in London in early October, Bourke-White photographed Winston Churchill, who had just been appointed minister of war, and Haile Selassie, emperor of Ethiopia, who, as legend has it, courteously helped carry Bourke-White's cameras to the elevator when their picture session in his modest London hotel room was completed.

Bourke-White's stay abroad was extended for several months to include coverage in Rumania,

Turkey, Egypt, and Syria. The trip was the sort of assignment that would seem to represent everything Bourke-White could possibly have wanted from her line of work. But early in February 1940, while Bourke-White was in Turkey staying at the Ankara Palace Hotel, she wrote a long letter to Erskine Caldwell, in which she conveyed startling feelings of dismay about her relationship with *Life*. She was "terribly low," she said, because of two blows that had befallen her at once that made her feel that the magazine was treating her "pretty shabbily."

» The first was to come here to the capital and start to make arrangements for official portraits and find that a *Life*-assigned photographer had preceded me by six weeks, made appointments with all the leading big-wigs which bans me from making them, even to a day in the home of the President, the hardest thing to get in any country.

I could not believe that he wasn't an imposter, until I cabled New York for an explanation and it was true enough, he was passing through here on other photographic business. He's not a staff member, of course, but a Swiss photographer and I guess they assigned him before they knew I was going here. Nothing the matter with that of course, but why couldn't they have told me? Letting me walk right into such a ridiculous situation, even to wiring me an identical detail of the assignment like the day with the President, and, of course, it means that when all my hard work is done, it won't mean anything because all my pictures will be mixed up with his, and no chance for a credit. . . . They've got to realize the seriousness of these things and stand behind their staff people better. «

The other blow was somewhat similar, although in a different form. While in London, Bourke-White had worked throughout one night without any sleep taking a series of pictures of life during a blackout. She was very proud of the series, which she felt provided a cross-section of London.

The photos were supposed to appear in the January 1, 1940, issue of *Life*, and Bourke-White was aghast when she received her copy of the issue in Ankara and discovered that there was only one tiny picture of hers in the midst of a layout of other night pictures. She felt the other pictures in the layout were good, and that the layout as a whole was well executed. "I don't know where the right and wrong of this is," she wrote to Caldwell. "All I know is that it makes me feel pretty futile to put so much inspiration into a story which seems to me to make a pretty good complete whole as I have planned it and executed it and to see such small driblets ever reach the light, and makes me feel still more useless because one more syndicate picture could have taken up the 4″ x 6″ that mine occupied without hurting the layout."

Simultaneously, Bourke-White received a letter from a former managing editor of *Life*, Ralph Ingersoll, who had left Luce's employ to begin his own pictorial publication, the short-lived daily afternoon newspaper *PM*. Ingersoll told Bourke-White in his letter that he had just succeeded in obtaining financing from Marshall Field, and offered her a job. Bourke-White went so far as to cable Ingersoll for more information, and explained to Caldwell, in that long letter to him: "I never felt in a readier mood to throw over my present job. After all, since early September, when that Hudson River story ran, there hasn't been a thing in *Life* to justify my existence."

Bourke-White knew, however, that such things ran in cycles at *Life:* "every so often I get a wonderful play there," she wrote. But it did seem to her that for the great quantity of pictures she took for *Life*, she had rather little to show for it. "The new paper, I think, will use the pictures better, and it's such a lot of fun to work with something while it's still new."

Writing to Caldwell from Istanbul at the end of February, Bourke-White indicated that she had still not settled in her own mind whether to accept Ingersoll's offer. The fact that the new venture would be a gamble did not worry her particularly. There were many things she and Caldwell could do if *PM* failed—new books, for example. She did not want to enter a project that was doomed to fail, of course, but was willing to take a reasonable risk.

"The trouble is," she concluded, "they [*Life*] are too rich and can afford to be wasteful of someone who's supposed to be their Ace. But the so-called Ace has only so many years to live and doesn't want to see the pictures taken in any one of them buried forever. . . ."

When she returned to the United States in the spring of 1940, Bourke-White quit the *Life* staff and decided to gamble on working for *PM*, which began appearing on New York City newsstands during the month of June. Featuring pages packed with photo-layouts, *PM* competed primarily with other daily New York tabloids.

PM seemed to offer Bourke-White a more comprehensive outlet for her vast range of photo talents. But the promise was never fulfilled, partly because an unusual problem plagued *PM* in its first month of publication. An anonymous document was circulated through the offices of several New York newspapers, which claimed that *PM* staff members were either members of the Communist party or Communist sympathizers. Bourke-White's name appeared on the list along with those of most of the *PM* staff.

Ingersoll refuted those imputations in an article of his own that appeared in the July 12, 1940, issue of *PM*, and invited the FBI to investigate the matter. The FBI followed up on Ingersoll's invitation, and went so far as to open a dossier on Bourke-White herself (beginning in October 1940). Bourke-White continued to be the subject of an undercover FBI investigation for the next fifteen years. Her file (obtained by the author under the Freedom of Information Act) contains more than 200 pages of information about her activities, with particular emphasis on her affiliation with so-called Communist-front organizations.

The FBI viewed her alleged Communist affiliations as a serious matter. So grave, in fact, that on April 9, 1941, J. Edgar Hoover, the FBI director, ordered that Bourke-White's name be placed on the list of citizens who were to be taken under "custodial detention" in the event of a national emergency.

Bourke-White never knew she was under FBI surveillance. In any case, this incident was only one of many disappointments she experienced while associated with *PM*. In October 1940 Bourke-White concluded her work for Ingersoll and returned to work for *Life*, but on a free-lance basis. For the remainder of Bourke-White's career, *Life* magazine was the primary source of her photographic assignments and the principal outlet for her pictures. But Bourke-White was not a full-time *Life* staff member again until 1951.

Her first assignment upon returning to the *Life* fold in the fall of 1940 was a cross-country tour of the United States with Erskine Caldwell for the purpose of gathering as much Americana as she and her husband could find. *Life* eventually decided not to use the material, however, and the work Bourke-White and Caldwell produced on that trip became the basis of their next book: *Say, Is This the U.S.A.?*

Published in the spring of 1941, *Say, Is This the U.S.A.?* was the least successful of their three collaborations. *North of the Danube* may have lacked the dramatic focus of *You Have Seen Their Faces*, but at least it was based on an intriguing conflict which involved political and social issues of mounting significance. *Say, Is This the U.S.A.?* has no dramatic focus and no intriguing conflict. It has the overdramatized corniness of a college yearbook: Class of U.S.A.—1940.

After *Say, Is This the U.S.A.?*, Bourke-White and Caldwell stopped collaborating on book projects. Caldwell's *All Out on the Road to Smolensk* and Bourke-White's *Shooting the Russian War* emerged from their next trip together.

Bourke-White had an urge to photograph World War II as early as 1933—an ambition she began to realize in 1938, when she witnessed the rising tide of world conflict in Czechoslovakia, and continued to realize when she immersed herself in photographing England and the Mideast preparing for war during the winter of 1939/40. Finally, in the spring of 1941, Bourke-White fulfilled her desire to photograph war itself.

She and Caldwell had a "joint and urgent conviction" that the Soviet Union's entrance into the war against Germany was imminent, and early in 1941 they laid plans to travel together to Russia to be present for the world-shattering events they were certain were about to unfold.

One of the few people who knew of their plans was Wilson Hicks, *Life*'s photography editor. Hicks shared their conviction that Russia would be the next key country in the march of the war, and assigned Bourke-White to the story for *Life*. Caldwell made no advance commitments, although he did have an understanding with *Life* and CBS radio to provide material if he got around to it. In fact, Caldwell and Bourke-White made historic shortwave broadcasts from Moscow to the United States, which were aired live over the CBS network during the summer of 1941.

Since most of Europe had fallen to the Germans by the spring of 1941, Bourke-White and Caldwell were forced to take the long route to the Soviet Union, by way of the Pacific Ocean, through China, finally entering the USSR by the back door, as it were, at Alma-Ata. On the first leg of their journey they made brief stops in Honolulu, Midway, Wake,

Madame Chiang Kai-shek, Chungking, 1941.

Guam, Manila, and Hong Kong; then they flew from Hong Kong to Chungking, the provisional capital of China, where Bourke-White had her first confrontation with the war during a Japanese air raid. The Chungking air raid, however, was mild indeed compared to the German air raids she would soon experience in Moscow.

While in Chungking, Bourke-White and Caldwell met Madame and Generalissimo Chiang Kai-shek, and at Madame Chiang's urging Bourke-White visited the Chungking "warphanage." China's homes for children orphaned by the war cared for over 30,000 youngsters, and the Chungking home, with school and living facilities combined, was representative of the "warphanages" that operated in every region of China during the war with Japan.

From Chungking, Bourke-White and Caldwell proceeded to the Soviet Union. They had to stop en route because of plane trouble in Lanchow, Suchow, and in an unknown location in the Gobi desert. Once beyond the Gobi they stopped in Hami, in the province of Sinkiang, and finally reached Alma-Ata on the Soviet border with China. One and a half days of flying later, they were in Moscow, having traveled fifteen thousand miles, almost two-thirds of the distance around the world, in a total flying time of one hundred hours.

At the beginning of May 1941, when Bourke-White and Caldwell arrived in Moscow, the non-aggression pact between Germany and the USSR was still in effect. Germans were to be seen in all the leading hotels; and, as Bourke-White observed, the government-controlled Soviet press did not contain a single anti-German word.

Bourke-White and Caldwell remained in Moscow for a month of bizarrely cold weather, and in early June, after obtaining permission to travel, the two left for an extended trip through the wheat fields of the Ukraine and to Kharkov, Rostov, the Donbas coal region, the Caucasus, and the Black Sea.

They had just flown into Sukhumi, a resort town on the Black Sea, hoping to enjoy a few days of rest and swimming after nearly a month of solid traveling, when the first news of war on Russian soil came over the town's loudspeaker. The date was Sunday, June 22, 1941. Bourke-White wrote: "Molotov had spoken from the Kremlin. Before daybreak, German planes had flown over the Soviet border and dropped bombs on Kharkov, Kiev, and other Soviet cities. Troops were being rushed to the border, and the indications were that the most intense warfare in history had begun."

It took Bourke-White and Caldwell five days to return to Moscow from Sukhumi. When they arrived there no longer were any Germans to be found in their hotel. The "fascist bandits," as the Russians called them, had all left during the week prior to the outbreak of war without paying their bills.

The two American correspondents were given one of the suites of lavish rooms recently vacated by a Nazi official. The suite cost no more than their previous quarters in the hotel, and had one feature that was immensely appealing to Bourke-White: a balcony.

"Opposite us was the Kremlin, Lenin's Tomb, and the Red Square—a magnificent Moscow panorama. If the *Luftwaffe* did any work on the Kremlin, I knew we would have the best viewpoint in the city to photograph it," Bourke-White wrote. The chambermaid told them that Trotsky had stood on that balcony addressing the unheeding trade unions at the

time of his fall from power. Lindbergh had also stayed in that suite during his visit to Moscow.

As far as Bourke-White could tell, the stage was set for some unusually exciting photographic work. But she woke up one morning to find that the military authorities had issued a *ukase* (decree) proclaiming that anyone seen with a camera would be shot on sight.

» Here was I, facing the biggest scoop of my life, an opportunity so great that a photographer would conceive it only in an opium dream: the biggest country enters the biggest war in the world, and I was the only photographer, on the spot, representing any publication and coming from any foreign country.

The anticamera law was decidedly inconvenient. But I had only to reflect on the supreme convenience of being within the country's borders at all, at a time when all sorts of other news photographers were hammering vainly on the gates, to be willing to face almost any difficulty, even that of shotguns. I did think, however, that to have to face German bombing planes and Russian firing squads on the same side of the same war was rather a lot for even a photographer to do. «

A greater inconvenience than the military law banning photographers was the threat of evacuation. The American ambassador to Moscow, Laurence Steinhardt, called Bourke-White and Caldwell to the Embassy to warn them of the perils they would face in the event of attack. The United States, Steinhardt insisted, might not be able to ensure their safety. Apparently their evacuation was already being reported in the American press, and *Life* was cabling in panic trying to determine the whereabouts of their photographer. The magazine's fears dismayed Bourke-White: "Surely, I thought, anybody would know that I would start throwing my lenses like hand grenades at anyone who tried to carry me away from such a scoop as this."

Ambassador Steinhardt agreed to help once Bourke-White and Caldwell showed their resolve to stay and cover the war. And the Soviet government relented also, issuing Bourke-White a special photographer's pass on July 15—just in time for the first German air raid on Moscow, which Bourke-White recorded from her hotel balcony.

The Moscow air raids were awesome, but there was a great deal more that interested Bourke-White besides the dazzling and suspenseful incendiary battles that nightly terrorized the city. Deeply significant changes had occurred in Russian society in the nearly ten years since Bourke-White had last visited the Soviet Union. During her six-month stay in 1941 Bourke-White could not help noticing some of the more recent developments. She discovered, for instance, the appearance everywhere of gigantic statues of Joseph Stalin.

» These tower above the populace in post offices, banks, hotel lobbies, universities, parks, and factory lunchrooms.... Where there is not room for a statue, a prominent wall is usually covered with a banner picturing the familiar mustached face in profile....

These representations gave me a curious feeling about Stalin. He is so seldom seen, so rarely heard, and yet so much quoted that one comes to think of him as an ever-present yet fleshless spirit, a kind of superman so big that no human frame can hold him, so powerful that everything down to the smallest action is guided by him.

Every time I walked into a public building and was startled afresh by one of those towering marble statues, my determination increased to obtain the difficult permission to photograph Stalin. I wanted to get that massive legendary face on a sheet of panchromatic film, focused through my own lens, to see if he then would look real or superhuman. «

With some help from Ambassador Harry Hopkins, whom President Roosevelt sent to Moscow on a good-will mission when war broke out, Bourke-White was given the opportunity to photograph Joseph Stalin. The unusual portrait session took place in Stalin's Kremlin office. In person, Stalin seemed very human to Bourke-White, particularly because he was about two inches shorter than she. At one point, Bourke-White had to crouch on her knees in order to make an exposure from a particularly low angle. The Soviet dictator was amused at the sight of an American woman assuming that position in his presence, and he began to laugh.

» When his face lighted up with a smile, the change was miraculous. It was as

Harry L. Hopkins, head of the U.S. Lend-Lease program, with Stalin in Moscow, 1941.

though a second personality had come to the front, genial, cordial, and kindly. I pressed on through two more exposures, until I had the expression that I wanted.

I got ready to go, and threw my stuff back into the camera case; then I noticed a peculiar thing about Stalin's face. When the smile ended, it was as though a veil had been drawn over his features. Again he looked as if he had been turned into granite, and I went away thinking that this was the strongest, most determined face I had ever seen. «

Between 1936 and 1941, as we now know, Stalin systematically purged those Russians who represented potential opposition to his regime. Although Bourke-White did not go so far as to accuse Stalin of the millions of murders he ordered carried out against his enemies, many of whom were leading cultural and intellectual figures in Russia, she was not so naïve as to overlook the chilling transformation that Stalin's reign had caused.

» The unity of the Soviet people has been assured because whatever dissention existed during the last few years was wiped out. Thus no organized opposition is left. These drastic measures offer another explanation of why there is no fifth-column movement in the country—one secret of the Soviet Union's strength. But the all-sweeping corrective measures which were taken did leave a wake of fear. Even among the patriotic and loyal, this fear was noticeable.

It was quite evident, for example, when we arrived before the outbreak of war. Ten years before, during my previous visits, the spirit of experimentation was everywhere. It was noticeable in all walks of life, but especially in creative fields, such as the theater. Many of the creative efforts were clumsy and crude, but they were always interesting because the germ of trial and discovery was there.

When I returned in the spring of 1941 I found that a crystallization had taken place. There was less of that refreshing experimentation with new things, and more conformity. No one could afford to make a mistake in ideology. «

That was probably as bold a statement about Soviet repression as any patriotic American writing in 1942 could make. *Shooting the Russian War* was published in 1943, and because the Russians were our allies, published comments had to place the Soviet regime in the best possible light for American eyes. Until the Cold War began, our staunch allies the Russians were our brothers in battle against the Nazis; the Soviet leader, "Uncle Joe" Stalin, was our friend.

Bourke-White carefully observed the shifts that occurred in the Russian people's attitudes under the stresses of war: the sudden sense of national unity, the fervent patriotism, the urge to work exceedingly hard for a cause that had reached life-or-death limits. Everyone in the Soviet Union seemed to want to accomplish achievements of heroic stature—the women in particular.

» During those first dramatic weeks of the war, you could go into any factory, and side by side with almost every man there was a woman standing. Sometimes it was his wife, sometimes it was his sweetheart; or it might be a woman brought from a less important industry; but the man was teaching that woman his job. Realizing that it is not an easy thing to take over a skilled job, the women were going to night school to increase their factory technique. They took great pride in keeping production up to the level that had been maintained by their husbands and brothers. «

Bourke-White was heartened most of all by the Russians' awareness of the purpose for which they were fighting. They were, of course, defending their homes against a brutal aggressor. But beyond the immediate goal of self-preservation, Bourke-White heard evidence of a broader understanding of what the war was all about.

A few days after the first German invasion, for instance, Bourke-White and Caldwell witnessed the following scene at the October Railroad Station.

» The freight yard was jammed with locomotive engineers and mechanics, rallying for active and reserve service in the army. A red-draped tribune had been hastily set up at the end of the yard, and a brakeman was calling through a megaphone, "We volunteer to fight not only for the life of our fatherland but for the whole of progressive humanity." «

Similarly, at the Stalin Auto Works, they saw one of the foremen jump to a platform and shout: "The motors we turn out shall be better than those of our enemy, for ours are made by free men, and theirs by slaves."

Bourke-White also had the opportunity to interview captured German soldiers, an experience that starkly illuminated the contrasts between the Russian and the German mentality. "The German captives had impressed me by their resemblance to animals," Bourke-White wrote.

» I suppose prisoners always appear at a disadvantage, and allowances should be made, but these German soldiers gave me the feeling that the Nazis were throwing into battle every man capable of supporting the weight of a gun. They were immature, half-baked young boys, with no ideas of their own, with no enthusiasm for anything. The fervid Führer-worship that we hear about may exist, but it was something I never saw. Neither did I see hatred. I observed only a blind acceptance of the job that had been mapped out for them. It was a job they disliked. They would rather have been home.

As things stood, they were glad to be warm and comfortable, with a handful of Russian cigarettes within reach. But their minds were the minds of automatons. There must be higher caliber soldiers than this, but I had the feeling that all available man power, down to the last dregs, was being poured into the Russian war. Perhaps what I was seeing was typical of a whole new generation which has grown up, pressed into a stifling mold. This, perhaps, is one of the most serious aspects of war and eternal readiness for war. «

One wounded German infantryman, whom Bourke-White interviewed in a Moscow hospital after the battle of Smolensk in early August, said: "It seems to me to be necessary to fight, but I do not know the reasons why. This is up to the officers. I am too small a man to know. . . ."

Bourke-White herself abhorred Nazi racism and repression. She was sensitized, as the average American at that time was not, to the enormous political and social ramifications of World War II, and she brought that sensitivity to bear in the passion for inquiry and understanding that distinguished her journalistic work throughout the 1940s. Each successive assignment enlarged Bourke-White's powers of observation and accordingly increased her gift for communicating her experiences. In the 1940s Bourke-White made writing an intrinsic facet of her professional work, a significant departure from earlier years, when she viewed writing as merely an adjunct to her photography. Only through writing, Bourke-White found, could she convey a comprehensive picture of the historic events she was privileged to witness. Writing also helped her integrate her experiences, providing a means for her psyche to absorb the excitements, dangers, and other startling phenomena that had become a regular part of her professional life.

In fact, many of the horrors with which she came in contact were too awful to think about while in the process of photographing them and she had to shield her thoughts and emotions when necessary.

On their way to the Russian war front in September 1941, Bourke-White and Caldwell spent one night in Vyazma. They were traveling with a group of international correspondents, which included Cyrus Sulzberger of *The New York Times*, Henry Cassidy of the Associated Press, Wallace Carroll of United Press International, and others.

Every night the reporters would gather together with their Russian hosts for lavish banquets. Their repast in the Vyazma International Hotel included saucers of sour cream with caviar and excellent small steaks served with slices of raw fish and raw onions. After washing all the food down with vodka, they went to bed, agreeing that the party was to rise promptly at half past six the next morning, to begin another leg of their journey to the front.

"I am always skeptical about these early-morning arrangements," Bourke-White wrote, "and anyone who takes photographs has had, I am sure, the same experience as I: that the people who are not photographers never realize the value of every hour of daylight. I didn't think all the vodka the night before would help matters either."

» Nevertheless, Erskine and I were up at six-thirty. As I had feared, everyone else was still sleeping, and neither of us could think of any polite way of waking up a lot of newspapermen and Russian officers. Ten minutes later the two of us were standing in the narrow hallway of our primitive little hotel while Erskine shaved in an affair which looked like a kitchen sink, the one source of running water in the hotel. I was waiting my turn behind him with my toothbrush when suddenly we heard it: the old familiar whine through the air. I was standing at a window, but I jumped away, grabbed Erskine by the shoulder, and in a second we were lying on the floor of the hall.

That first of several bombs that fell had one practical result. It brought everybody out of bed. All the doors down the length of the hallway opened simultaneously, as though pulled by a single string, and correspondents came plunging out on their hands and knees in various stages of scanty attire. One member of our party did not appear, and when the bombing stopped we went into his room and looked at him. It was the censor, and he was lying in bed, unhurt, but completely surrounded by the window sash, which had fallen in on him so precisely that he looked like a picture in a frame.

I was dressed, fortunately, and I snatched up my camera and ran out into the street. The air reeked with the smell of cordite. After a bomb drops, the atmosphere for some minutes is filled with a peculiar cloud. Bits of plaster, dust, and crumbled brick hang so thickly in the air that it is a little time before one can see just what has happened. I could

Margaret Bourke-White in 1943. Photograph by Alfred Eisenstaedt.

little courtyard it lifted enough to reveal a sight that until then had been veiled. A family of four lay in their doorway, in contorted positions and very still. I set down the dog and began taking pictures.

It is a peculiar thing about pictures of this sort. It is as though a protecting screen draws itself across my mind and makes it possible to consider focus and light values and the technique of photography, in as impersonal a way as though I were making an abstract camera composition. This blind lasts as long as it is needed—while I am actually operating the camera. Days later, when I developed the negatives, I was surprised to find that I could not bring myself to look at the films. I had to have someone else handle and sort them for me.

As I worked, a woman ran up and sank to the ground by the mangled body of a young girl with dust-filled yellow hair, one of the bombed group. I learned from the comments around me that this was her mother. She had been down the street when the bombs fell, and this was the first she knew that her daughter had been killed. Her desperate moans penetrated even my protective shell, and as I focused my camera on this vision of human misery it seemed heartless to turn her suffering into a photograph. But war is war and it has to be recorded.

A larger rescue squad arrived with a truck and shovels. The shreds of blood and hair and internal organs and clothing were scraped up and thrown into the truck, and it removed one more small family that had taken its unconscious stand between Hitler and his *Lebensraum.* «

In early October, after returning to Moscow from the Yelnya front, Bourke-White and Caldwell completed their circumnavigation of the globe. To begin their journey home, they obtained passage on an 11,000-ton British troop ship, one of twenty-two vessels that had left Archangel Harbor on a fifteen-day-long convoy through the White Sea, the Barents Sea, the Arctic Ocean, the Norwegian and North seas, finally landing in Glasgow, Scotland.

One week later Bourke-White and Caldwell were in London, where they took part in a BBC broadcast to occupied Europe, "so as to let the enslaved nations know what was going on in Russia," Bourke-White wrote. In the booth next to theirs, in the subcellar the BBC had been using since its building was bombed, General de Gaulle was also talking to occupied Europe.

tell that several buildings directly across the street from our hotel had been demolished, and I started to walk into the flying cloud when I saw something moving toward me. It was a little white puppy, and I marveled that he had come out alive. I picked him up and held him in my arms; I could feel him trembling with fear. Rescue squads were arriving now, most of them girls in the uniforms of medical sisters, and they started searching the wreckage. Four of them climbed over a pile of clapboard that had recently been a house and reappeared, carrying a stretcher between them. On it lay the body of an old man, so covered with powdered plaster that he looked like the unfinished work of a sculptor. The beard and eyebrows seemed to have been merely indicated with a few rough chisel strokes. And then, so suddenly that the girl rescuers were as startled as I, he sat up on his stretcher.

It made me happy that the man and the dog were alive, and I pressed on into the ruins. The plaster cloud was still whirling, and as I walked into a

From London, Bourke-White and Caldwell took off for Bristol, "A scarred patch of desolation," Bourke-White wrote, "more completely wrecked block for block than London." As they entered the devastated town, air-raid sirens began wailing. Bristol, which had been quiet for months, was bombed as soon as they reached the city.

Bourke-White and Caldwell flew to Portugal the next morning, briefly stopping en route in Barcelona. From Lisbon they flew to the Azores, on to Bermuda, and arrived home in New York for Sunday dinner on October 20. Bourke-White was back on the road in no time, however. Less than twenty-four hours following her return to New York she was facing her first lecture audience.

Bourke-White lectured about her Russian trip up and down the East Coast almost nonstop for most of November, broke for most of December and January, and continued lecturing through major cities all over the United States in February and March. One of the public-speaking engagements she had in the early part of this lecturing period was a panel discussion on the topic of national health care in the United States. The panel, in which Eleanor Roosevelt also participated, was sponsored by a group called "Town Meeting" at facilities provided by Columbia University in New York City.

Bourke-White's comments on that occasion prove that despite the range of her foreign experiences, she was still deeply concerned about the condition of American society.

» If our democracy is going to continue, it must provide for the people as well as if not better than the totalitarian states do in terms of certain basic commodities: healthful conditions, adequate education and economic welfare. . . .

Our country lacks some of the aspects of democracy when colored people who must pay taxes as regularly as their white neighbors derive such dissimilar benefits. It lacks some of the advantages which might be expected of a democracy when great masses of people, in their ignorance and poverty, spend their insufficient pennies on patent medicines or on snuff, instead of benefiting from a system of medical and hospitalization insurance, which would ensure them proper care when needed. «

When it came to the question of leadership in world affairs, Bourke-White was a staunch advocate

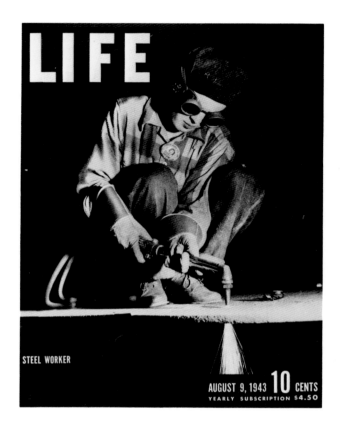

of the United States, despite the domestic problems she knew the country faced. Between 1941 and 1945 there were no issues of greater consequence for humanity than the moral and strategic battles the United States and her allies had to win in World War II, and those battles henceforth became Bourke-White's chief concerns. Also, since World War II was the most dramatic event at that time, Bourke-White was drawn instinctively to witnessing and recording as many scenes of the conflict as she could, no matter what trials she had to endure in the process.

One of the first crises of the war for Bourke-White was a personal one: her marriage broke up. The final separation seems to have been provoked by a simple, unbreachable difference in plans. Early in 1942 Caldwell secured a Hollywood writing job for himself and an offer for Bourke-White as well, and proposed that they move to Arizona, where he had just bought a ranch. All of that sounded to Bourke-White like a "set of golden chains." She was not interested in sitting idly in Arizona or Hollywood,

Autographing a bomb in a B-17, England, 1942.

while history was being made overseas. There was no alternative, as far as Bourke-White could see, but to call it quits. So ended their five-year working relationship. There was no bitterness. Another door slammed shut and Bourke-White drove on.

When the United States entered the war in 1941, Bourke-White was very eager to become a war correspondent and prevailed upon *Life* magazine to obtain military accreditation for her from the Pentagon and the U.S. Air Force. Under the agreement that was made, both *Life* and the Pentagon would be able to use Bourke-White's pictures. However, since the Air Force had never before accredited a woman as a war correspondent, a new uniform had to be designed. Bourke-White happily served as the model for the Army War College's team of uniform designers; Abercrombie & Fitch did the final stitching, and thereafter uniforms for female war correspondents followed the pattern created for Bourke-White.

Duly accredited and uniformed, Bourke-White was soon off on her first assignment: to England in the summer of 1942. Her arrival at a small, secret air base outside London coincided with that of the first thirteen heavy bombers (B-17's) that the U.S. Air Force had sent to begin the raids in Germany.

While at the bomber base, Bourke-White was permitted to take pictures of almost everything, but no matter how often she asked, she was never allowed to go on an actual bombing mission. For many months no one from the press was given per-

mission to fly with a crew in action. Then the rule was changed, and male reporters began to go. Technically, Bourke-White should have been allowed also, since recording an actual raid was vital to her assignment. But she knew that the brass feared criticism lest something happen to a woman photographer.

Very soon, however, the gentlemen's agreement barring Bourke-White from accompanying a B-17 crew in flight landed her in truly desperate waters. In early winter 1942, when the North African campaign began and the press corps boarded Flying Fortresses for the trip across the Mediterranean to cover the new front, it was decided that Bourke-White take the safer route, by convoy. The upshot was that the male reporters who flew reached their destination without incident, while Bourke-White's convoy was torpedoed by the Germans.

Although the sinking of her ship en route to Algiers was one of the most frightening moments in Bourke-White's life, it had one practical outcome. When she arrived in North Africa, General Jimmy Doolittle gave her permission to go on a bombing mission, saying, "Well, you've been torpedoed, you may as well go through everything."

General Doolittle relayed his okay to General Atkinson, commanding officer of the 97th Bomber Group in the Sahara, and on January 22, 1943, Bourke-White became the first woman ever to accompany an Air Force crew on a bombing mission.

Although Bourke-White devoted two brief chapters in *Portrait of Myself* to her adventures with the 97th Bomber Group in the Sahara, nothing captures the immediacy of her excitement quite as memorably as do her original notes, which she took at the time of the mission itself. Out of the series of fragments, snatches of conversation, and fleeting impressions Bourke-White scribbled in her notebook, a vivid record of the mission emerges.

THE BRIEFING

» We were on our way toward what was to be the greatest experience of my life. After six months of begging it was decided that I had earned my spurs working with U.S. Air Forces and could go on a bombing mission over enemy territory. I was the first woman ever to be allowed such a privilege. I was very proud.

The commanding general (Atkinson), one of the youngest in the service, would lead the raid. He is a tall lanky cowboy from Texas, and has had more actual combat than any other general in our air service. A superb flier, he frequently leads the missions himself. This was to be his fourteenth. . . .

I had listened and taken photographs often during briefings, but it was with a different feeling that I slipped in among the combat crews today. I was one of them. I was going to take the same risks that they took. **«**

The day's target was an important one: the El Ouina airfield, near Tunis harbor, which the Germans were using in ferrying troops across from Sicily. Bourke-White flew in the lead ship with General Atkinson piloting. The co-pilot, Paul Tibbetts, was a man with an ominous destiny ahead of him: in August 1945 Tibbetts piloted the P-29 *Enola Gay*, which dropped the first atom bomb on Hiroshima.

EARLY ON MISSION

» Finally I got established in one spot where the waist gunner could plug me into the interphone system. Spoke through the phone mike to make sure I was correctly connected. I heard the General's voice, "Repeat that!" "This is Margaret. I wanted to make sure I was plugged in OK." "Clear as a bell."

Turning from one side to another I had to be careful about the many long cords—tangled up like a barber pole. I had an extra extension on my oxygen, but that was still not long enough to carry me all the places I wanted to go. The portable oxygen bottle was good for about three minutes, the number of minutes seemed pretty short. . . .

NEAR TARGET

So reassuring when approaching target. Everyone saying OK, everything is OK. They check with each other, with other ships. OK.

Bombardier pulling pins out of the bombs. Tabs in his mouth. Didn't know I was sneaking up on him. When I took flash pictures he thought the bombs were exploding in his hands.

As we approached target, people running, people in trucks and they were really moving.

Tossup with the gunner over who would win his

Ready for a flying mission, 1943.

window seat—him or me? Didn't warn him that you trained yourself pushing the newsreel men out of the way.

The majesty of it, the rendezvous. Ancient Carthage lay below. Catching the glint of the backlight on the salt lake, now a marsh. We were wheeling in now the bomb run.

"I'm going to work first on this side, and then swing to the other waist window," I told the waist gunner. The tail gunner had forgotten that there was a woman on board and nearly jumped out when he heard my voice, I was told later.

The cloud bank over the Mediterranean Sea moving in.

Dallas ship, *Peggy D*, etched against the clouds. . . .

OVER TARGET

Rhythmic, like music, and so reassuring. The majesty of it, the formation of great planes sweeping up to the target.

21,000 feet: bomb to ground 35 sec. Moving forward four miles a minute.

Everyone else in formation sees our doors open. They know we're about to hit the Initial Point. This next turn will be the turn on to the target. Next communication is "Bombs Away." Each a split fraction of a second after the other. Ninety tons dropped on Tunis by thirty fortresses.

Pilot: "Close the bomb bay doors."

Bombardier: "Doors closed, OK to turn."

Pilot acknowledges with click of mike only and immediately takes sharp turn and evasive action—either losing or gaining altitude simultaneously.

Then we look back and hope to see a lot of fires.

LEAVING THE TARGET

Bombardier keeps watching the target. Then the bursts start showing up. You'd see initial explosions, then a little jet of fire licking out, then explosions would spread burning gas to other planes parked; pretty soon the whole thing is an inferno.

As a photographer, I would have liked to be in two places at once: in the sky where I was, and on the ground photographing a fire 5,000 feet high.

During the rally of the formation after the bombing run Pilot to gunners: "Bandit at 6 o'clock. Repeat. Bandit at 6 o'clock."

All gunners state: "OK."

The enemy plane we saw first never did close in. Gunners were checking among themselves: "Can you hear me?"

Top turret shot one fighter down. "He was head on into us. Only 20 yards away. They don't paint names on their airplanes or we'd have read them. They were making pass after pass, right smack in the nose."

Turret: "He didn't putter. Was on him like a duck after a lady bug."

AFTERWARD

"How was it? Were you excited?"

"No," I said, trying to imitate the pilots I heard so often. "It was routine. Quite routine."

I felt a little cheated. No fighter attacks within camera range.

"Yes there were plenty," the General said. The group behind us shot them down, but I didn't see it.

The flak was late. "That's the way I like it," said the General, "as close as I like to see it. . . ."

INTELLIGENCE REPORT

Bombing results were unusually good. Ten to fifteen large fires with black smoke, with several severe explosions emitting white smoke.

"Doesn't anyone want to interrogate me?" I asked.

They laughed. "We want to see your pictures." And sure enough my pictures were the only ones to show the fires. «

———

Bourke-White returned to the United States in the spring of 1943. After a few months of rest, she and Wilson Hicks got together to decide on her next assignment. "I'd like to see the war on the ground," Bourke-White told Hicks. "I'd like to photograph artillery. And see what the Engineers are doing. And there must be dozens of things that go on to make up a war that our American public doesn't know much about."

Around that time, a request for Bourke-White's services came from the Army Service Forces in the War Department. Under General Brehon Somervell, the ASF was accomplishing an enormous supply job, which fact had failed to reach the attention of most Americans. As Bourke-White explained:

» Sixty per cent of the war was a matter of supplying our troops with food, ammunition, medical and even spiritual services (the latter under chaplains). All this was the result of a chain-belt system which girdled the world—reaching from our factories to the front lines, according to a process known to the Service Forces as "logistics." But to most American people, "logistics," if they ever heard it, was just a word. That was where I came in. From their headquarters in the Pentagon Building, the ASF issued a request that I go overseas with our Army to show how supplies are brought to our troops: to tell in photographs the great story of "logistics." «

———

The logistics assignment pleased *Life* because they could show in pictures that "It's a Big War," the title they subsequently gave to one series of pictures Bourke-White turned out during her assignment (*Life*: January 10, 1944).

Bourke-White herself was delighted with the opportunity because she would have a chance to follow up many of the subjects in which she was most interested.

» Having always liked industrial photography, I was eager to portray the Engineers. ASF, in addition to Engineers and

Quartermaster, included Medical Corps, Transportation, Signal Corps, WAC's, Chaplains, and Ordnance. Through Ordnance, I would reach Artillery. Through many of these diversified activities I would reach the soldier at the front and picture his activities from a new point of view. The focal point of all this gigantic system of service and supply was the front-line soldier, and that was the story I wanted to tell in pictures. «

This was also the assignment that brought Bourke-White into her stride as a writer.

» The very intimacy of the Italian conflict sharpened my awareness of human beings, and I began to listen to what people said. I mean really listen. Someone drops a phrase and you say to yourself, "No one else could have said just that thing in just that way. It is like a portrait of the man." Until then, I had considered myself eye-minded and let it go at that, but much as I love cameras, they can't do everything. The American soldier with his bitter humor and his peculiar gallantry had opened my ears.

There was a haunting quality about that phase of the war, with all those American boys against the unfamiliar background of "Sunny Italy." I tried whenever possible to capture the special flavor of a situation in words as well as pictures. If a GI in the photograph I was taking made some pungent remark, I jotted it down. . . . The important thing was to get the words down while they were fresh in memory. Most of these notes had to be made on the fly, since we were always tearing in mad haste from one spot to another, and that meant writing on my knees while the Jeep bucked and pitched over the muddy, disintegrating roads. . . .

Sometimes, there would be only two or three wildly scrawled letters on a page, or a single syllable. But no matter how unreadable it was, the sight of those scribbles would evoke the situation and the people in it. As the jottings piled up, I could see that sooner or later this was going to be a book. «

In the spring of 1944 Bourke-White succeeded in turning her scribbled notes into *Purple Heart Valley*, a brilliant piece of writing, rich with suspense and insight, on the men and women of the Army Service Forces in Italy, and the prodigious tasks they were carrying out there.

She began in Naples, where underwater engineers were busy clearing the port for allied use, after the retreating Germans had sunk a harborful of ships—one on top of the other—so as to make the job of rebuilding the port of Naples as difficult as possible. From Naples, Bourke-White proceeded to the Fifth Army front, which throughout the winter of 1943–1944 was enclosed within a mountain triangle formed by the Cassino corridor, the hills behind Venafro, and the rugged terrain behind the little town of Colli.

Since the Germans held the highest peaks in the battle area, and thereby kept an open line of sight on all activities occurring below them, American troops in Cassino Valley worked under the constant threat of carefully placed enemy fire. Bourke-White could not avoid being subjected to numerous German shelling attacks, traveling as close to the front as she did on this assignment, and had more than one close call. Although she was never wounded, the shelling attacks took their toll on her nerves. On one of her return trips to Naples, after a particularly stiff period of Nazi shelling at the front, Bourke-White wrote:

» I find it difficult to express the blessed relief, the quickening joy, with which you find yourself heading home from the front. Each mile in the road brings a lightening of the heart. Every day I had felt this surge of relief when I started homeward, and I was not proud of it.

What was happening to me, I wondered. For the last several years, as a war correspondent, I had been through my quota of bombings. I had been bombed in Barcelona, in Chungking, in Great Britain, North Africa, and Moscow. And, while nobody likes having bombs come too close, on the whole I had not minded it too much. You are a small target in a big place, and the chances are that you will pull through. You are willing to take your gambling chances in a city.

But shelling was different. Shelling was like a dentist with a drill. And with me, those shells had found the nerve.

Partly I think it was knowing how much science went into the aiming of those guns that made it so hard to take. The enemy was after a specific target. If you were unlucky enough to be at that target, from your point of view he was after you. It was intensely horribly personal. . . .

As we drove homeward, I did a lot of wondering about how those boys felt who had to stay up there week after week, and sometimes month after month, without even the break of getting out of it for a night. Later I was to see the deathly strain on their faces, the growing numbness that enveloped them like a shroud. This numbness was their only defense against an anxiety that had become intolerable. To live in a state of mental paralysis was the only way they could stand it. **《**

Back in the comparative safety of Naples, Bourke-White was able to give careful consideration to the extraordinary aspect of life there. With people living in caves, hungry, confused, and often deathly ill, Neapolitan society had indeed taken on bizarre characteristics.

Bourke-White saw many good efforts to alleviate the desperate situation in Naples, but she also saw a lack of sufficient guidance on the part of the Allied Military Government, which had given rise to a serious black-market problem. "In the early weeks of the occupation, when submarines were still a factor to be reckoned with," Bourke-White wrote, "many American boys risked their lives to bring over these shiploads of food. It was unfortunate that muddled handling of supplies sometimes aggravated rather than cured the food problem."

No doubt, Bourke-White's critical observations were not the sort of publicity the Pentagon had reckoned with when they assigned her to cover the logistics story. *Life* certainly never conveyed Bourke-White's deeper insights to the American public. Typically, under Bourke-White's scrutiny, the problem of supplying occupied Italy raised more serious issues than the immediate symptoms of high prices and severe shortages of basic goods had brought to light.

» Our aid to the Italians operates like a giant breadline, and like all breadlines has a profound effect on the economy. We do not get automatic rewards for generosity unless it is employed with intelligence, and lack of intelligence is indicated by our failure to control the black market which the breadline has nurtured. If we choose to go in for breadline tactics, that breadline should be used as a sound political investment. If it is not, then a priceless opportunity will have been lost.

We Americans, moving on as a victorious army, have an opportunity to mold the world—an occasion almost unprecedented in history. Our soldiers buy that opportunity with the dearest possession they have. We have no right to ask them to lay down their lives unless we administer what they have gained with the full intelligence that their sacrifice deserves. **《**

As an ordnance officer says in *Purple Heart Valley:* "Straightening up this Italian situation is like trying to put toothpaste back into tubes"—a realistic assessment of the problem, which Bourke-White duly noted one morning while riding to the front. Bourke-White and the ordnance officer were in a Jeep crossing a pontoon bridge over the Volturno River.

» When we reached the opposite bank we were surrounded by children, chanting what has become almost the national song of Italy: *"Caramelle, caramelle."* We paused long enough to empty our pockets of the hard candies we always carried. An equitable distribution was impossible. It was painful to find ourselves the center of such a rush and scramble and laughter and tears, to have to hear the shouts of triumph and disappointed cries. I spotted one sad-faced mother at the side of the road, much too young for the two babies she carried, and I leaned out so she could safely reach the package of Lifesavers I still had intact. The heavenly smile that lighted her thin face showed what a prize it was to her to get the entire package.

"I can't stand it when it's kids. God, it's awful," said the ordnance officer as we drove on. "I lie awake nights and suffer just thinking about them. And the darn little rascals can even grin at you."

Around the next bend in the road we met another sight I found interesting and moving in a totally different way. A gang of Negro soldiers were stacking ammo into those neat grocery-store piles which dot the roadsides near the front. In charge of them was a fine-looking officer. I noticed the bright eyes in the intelligent ebony-colored face even before I observed that he wore captain's insignia.

We stopped for a few minutes here while the officer accompanying me hopped out to do some checking on the arrival of the ordnance supplies. While I sat in the Jeep waiting, I remembered some of the difficulties which, I had heard, confront Negroes who wish to increase their technical training while in the Army, and who seek to enter Officers' Candidate School. For this fellow to have risen to captain, I thought, he must be good.

The Negro troops who had been given the chance to work in forward areas, I reflected (and many of them had not been), had indeed earned their way. I had seen them doing Army service jobs all along the way from North Africa to Italy, stacking C rations, sorting worn clothes, working in road gangs, loading and unloading ships, and I had observed that they had done these jobs efficiently and well. Here, close to the battle zone, I had seen them transporting and handling ammunition stores along roads which represent selected German targets, where a shell hit on ammo costs the lives of all who handle it. I watched the colored captain moving briskly from group to group, directing the dispersal of the ammo load into widely separated piles, a precaution so that a direct shell hit will not blow up the whole countryside.

I had heard a good many discussions about whether Negroes could stand up under shell fire. What makes anybody stand up under shell fire, I wondered. Part of it is knowing what you're fighting for (if you know); part of it is certainly *esprit de corps*, that instinct not to let the gang down. There had been little opportunity back in the States for Negroes and white men to develop mutually that spirit of not letting the gang down. Perhaps mutual trial by fire would bring about one constructive gain from this war. Already Negro pilots, flying with the 93rd Division in the Pacific and the 99th Pursuit Squadron in Italy, had made a potent contribution in this direction. Their records as fighters had earned the respect of Allied fliers everywhere.

As I watched the colored ammo squad, under the competent direction of their young commanding officer, I reflected that we owe these Negro soldiers a great deal. Although many of them at home have had advantages unequal to ours, still they are working side by side with their fellow Americans in the hope that in this war they are earning first-class citizenship.

My ordnance officer finished his check and climbed into the Jeep. As we started on our way he turned to me and said something that made it hard to realize that this was the same man who had been so distressed half a mile back at the plight of the children. His remark was: "It makes my blood boil to see a nigger with bars on his shoulders." «

Bourke-White's sensitive antennae picked up much revealing information about the attitudes of American servicemen in Italy, and as was the case with the ordnance officer's comment, much of what she heard deeply troubled her.

One telling encounter began with Bourke-White's taking pictures of the Fifth Army's huge bread-baking operation. When she finished taking pictures, she turned to the group of GI's that surrounded her and plunged in with the question she felt every American could answer with at least some degree of understanding: "What are you fighting for?"

» "Funny you should ask us that," said the top sergeant. "We had an essay contest about that just a while ago."

"Tell her about the winning essay," said the others, chuckling.

"Well, the men were asked to write a composition as lengthy as could be. The subject: 'Why I'm Fighting.' The winning composition was very short—just six words: 'Why I'm fighting. I was drafted.' "

"Now tell me in more than six words," I said. . . .

"Because Germany has a different form of government. . . ."

"To protect our homes and our country. . . ."

"So we can get the war over quick and go home. . . ."

"Do you want to find things at home exactly the way you left them?" I asked. The answer to this one was easy. A chorus of voices assured me that merely getting home was all any man could ask. . . .

The question-and-answer program came to a halt with the return of Captain Ernest and the ordnance officer. My traveling companion was eager to get me on to a heavy maintenance depot, where a gun-tube change was in process. . . .

There was no doubt that these men felt a deep insecurity about their future in civilian life. They were worried about whether women in industry would be willing to hand their jobs back. They were deeply resentful toward organized labor without having much information about the issues. They felt they had a score to settle with those people who, while the boys were overseas, had been home "feathering their own nests. . . ."

"It isn't so much cash that the men want," the top sergeant concluded, as Padgitt* and I began to

*Padgitt was Bourke-White's technical assistant.

gather up the cameras and place them in the Jeep. "It's a job—a good job—with enough pay so we can buy a home, an automobile, and raise a family. Is that too much to ask?"

As the gun tube was finally eased onto the carriage, the human ballast jumped down to talk to me. It made me feel a bit self-conscious to go about all day asking soldiers what they were fighting for, but I was interested, so once more I plunged in.

A broad-shouldered master sergeant with ACE lettered on his helmet replied, "I don't suppose there's any man here would want to leave till it was all over and done with, but most of us want to get this mess cleaned up and go home."

"I suppose a lot of us are fighting for our wives and kids," said the pug-nosed test recorder.

"Hey, Bud, maybe you got kids," said Ace, "but I happen to know you ain't got no wife."

"Well, I can dream, can't I?" remarked Bud. "There's approximately forty million girls in America and all of them can't be smart."

"I guess there's lots of fellows fighting for babies they haven't seen," said the winch operator.

"That's my case," remarked a small-arms inspector. "The way my wife writes, she seems to expect our kid to talk, creep, and have teeth all at two months and six days. I tell her she must think she's got Superman, Jr."

"Write her to watch out or the draft board will be calling him for an interview," chuckled Bud.

"I'm one guy that's twice as bad off," said Ace, and the others laughed because Ace had recently become the father of twins.

"All right," I said. "You're fighting for the babies you have or the babies you hope to have. Anything else?"

"I can tell you what we ain't fighting for," volunteered an auburn-haired PFC they called Ruby. "We ain't fighting for none of those labor leaders."

"That's right," said the winch operator. "Let some of those jokers hear a few screaming meemies come whistling at them and they'd be glad to go back down into a nice deep coal mine."

"I know a lot of fellows that are going to react like that soldier we heard of that punched John L.'s face when he got back to the States," said Ruby. . . .

"How about most of the men you know over here?" I asked. "Does the average man do much thinking about whether there's a connection between our war aims and getting rid of Fascism?"

The small-arms inspector had been listening attentively and at this point he broke in with: "I don't think that's a subject for the average American to think about. . . ."

I had found the final statement of the small-arms inspector the most interesting of all. Why was it, I wondered, that the "average American" both in and out of the Army shrank from digging into the issues of this war when they concerned him so deeply. Some of them, like Ace, evidently had given the problem thought, but it was not the rule. I knew from my previous experience during the Russian war that all you had to do was to give the average Russian an opening and he would break into impassioned oratory on the subject. He would trace all the relationships as he saw them among book burnings, oppression of minorities, racial injustice, and war. The average Britisher would make shorter speeches, but would discuss articulately the issues of war and international politics. Even in Chungking, I had heard thoughtful and comprehensive opinions expressed by the Chinese.

And yet we were so clever and quick about everything else. The bakery and the heavy maintenance ordnance unit I had seen that day were two of the countless expert activities which make ours the best-fed and best-equipped army in the world. The same organizing ability which enabled us to establish hotel chains, bakery companies, mail-order houses, transportation and maintenance facilities to serve and supply our great territory of forty-eight states was being translated effectively into the organization of war. Maybe our accomplishments had made us smug.

Our Jeep came to a stop as the road dipped into a stream bed. A line of trucks spaced far back on the road was waiting to ford the stream. As we waited our turn, I noticed that a dead mule, which blocked a rivulet beside us, had built up its own little dam of muddy water. A large truck full of GI's started plunging across the flooded road. It got stuck in the middle and it took some time for the driver, with the help of a road gang, to negotiate the ford. This gave me an opportunity to study the faces of the human cargo the truck carried.

They were infantrymen returning to a bivouac area for rest, and I knew from the division emblem they wore on their sleeves that these men had been up in the mountains around Cassino for an unbroken sixty days.

I thought I had never seen such tired faces. It was more than the stubble of beard that told the story; it was the blank, staring eyes. The men were so tired that it was like a living death. They had come from such a depth of weariness that I wondered if they would ever be able quite to make the return to the lives and thoughts they had known. . . .

We drove on through the deepening dusk, with the guns spurting jagged flashes from every muddy glen and gully. I tried to imagine living for sixty days without once getting your shoes dry. It seemed to me that only one thing would make it possible to bear sixty days in soaking boots, sixty days of near-misses from screaming shells, and that was a support which many of these men did not have. The only way the human spirit could endure such torture unscathed was the deep, glowing knowledge of what the fight was for. «

As the preceding passages illustrate, Bourke-White was acutely interested in the United States serviceman's attitude toward the war. But *Purple Heart Valley* contains fewer records of thought than of action, and of the many impressive actions Bourke-White recounts in the book, not all were those performed by service*men*. Bourke-White spent several days on a story about the Fifth Army field hospital, where she was most strongly affected by the courage of the ten women working as surgical nurses there.

The films Bourke-White used to show the work of the Fifth Army medical team have never come to light, however. All the negatives were lost by the Pentagon en route through the censorship process. The loss remained one of the most painful experiences of Bourke-White's entire career, since there was absolutely no possibility for her to retake the pictures. But such disappointments notwithstanding, Bourke-White accrued considerable gains from her assignment in Italy—gains in experience, insight, and understanding which profoundly influenced her journalism.

In Italy, Bourke-White managed to acquire sufficient personal experience of the United States war activities to develop her own informed opinion on what was being done well and what was being done badly, or not at all. It was less an opinion than a plea she expressed; and of all her comments in *Purple Heart Valley*, perhaps the most lasting is Bourke-White's plea for the peaceful future she hoped the war would secure.

» In Italy, as on a greater scale in Germany, the effects of Fascism have left their mark on the minds of the people. The only way to leave constructive results behind us in these occupied countries—in fact, the only way to ensure future peace in the world—is through education of the young.

In Italy, it seemed to me, we were neglecting a magnificent opportunity. It was not enough to conquer this territory if we did not educate it in such a way that we could live at peace with it in the future. . . . Children were roaming the streets, sitting huddled in the caves and tunnels of Naples, growing up to a future of ignorance and prejudice. It mattered little whether the reasons for educating these waifs were humanitarian or based on hardheaded insurance for the future. They were growing up; why not take a hand in raising a future generation that would not bear arms against us, that would understand a democratic way of life?

If this is important in Italy, how much more important it will be when we get into Germany. There an educational job of colossal proportions will face us. It will be difficult, partly because we do not know just what we want to teach, and partly because we have had no practice. Italy could serve as a training ground for the great task that awaits us with Nazi-trained youth.

What is the use of all this bloodshed unless we insure the future for civilization and for peace? What is the use of leaving all these American boys behind on the battlefields, if we leave occupied countries unchanged when we move on? The fault begins not with our armies. The fault begins with us at home.

We are genuinely a freedom-loving people, and freedom is more than a word to us; but the added element of leadership is needed here. If we had a living political philosophy, if democracy were an articulate passion with us, we would be able to communicate it to others. There is no use fighting a war unless we leave behind us a better world, and to do that we must get the youth of Europe on our side. «

Former Hudson's Bay Company post manager Charles T. Gaudet, Fort Norman, N.W.T., Canada, 1937.

Mother Superior of the Sisters of Charity hospital, Fort Smith, N.W.T., Canada, 1937.

Flood victims, Louisville, Kentucky, 1937.

Taxi dancers, Fort Peck, Montana, 1936.

Czechoslovakian soldiers, 1938.

Farmer in Czechoslovakia, 1938.

Nazi rally, Reichenberg, Bohemia, 1938.

Skoda Works, Pilsen, Bohemia, 1938.

Hitler Youth, Moravia, 1938.

Talmud class, Czechoslovakia, 1938.

Arms drill at Eton College, England, 1939.

Tower Bridge during the blackout, London, 1940.

USSR, 1941.

USSR, 1941.

The Kremlin during a night air raid, 1941.

Awaiting rescue off North Africa, December 1942.

Air raid over Tunis, 1943.

Brigadier General Joseph Atkinson, North Africa, 1943.

Waist gunners, England, 1942.

Martha Raye entertaining troops in North Africa, 1943.

Harbor of Naples, 1944.

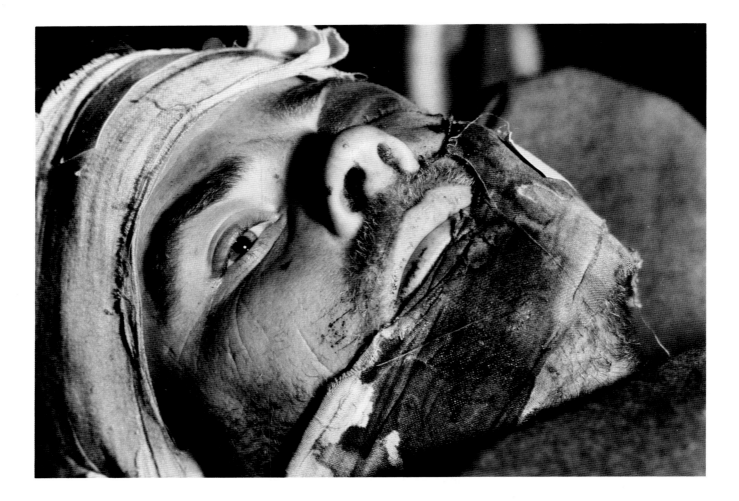

Wounded G.I., Cassino Valley, Italy, Winter 1943–44.

Lieutenant Colonel Paul W. Sanger operating in the 38th Evacuation Hospital, Cassino Valley, Winter 1943–44.

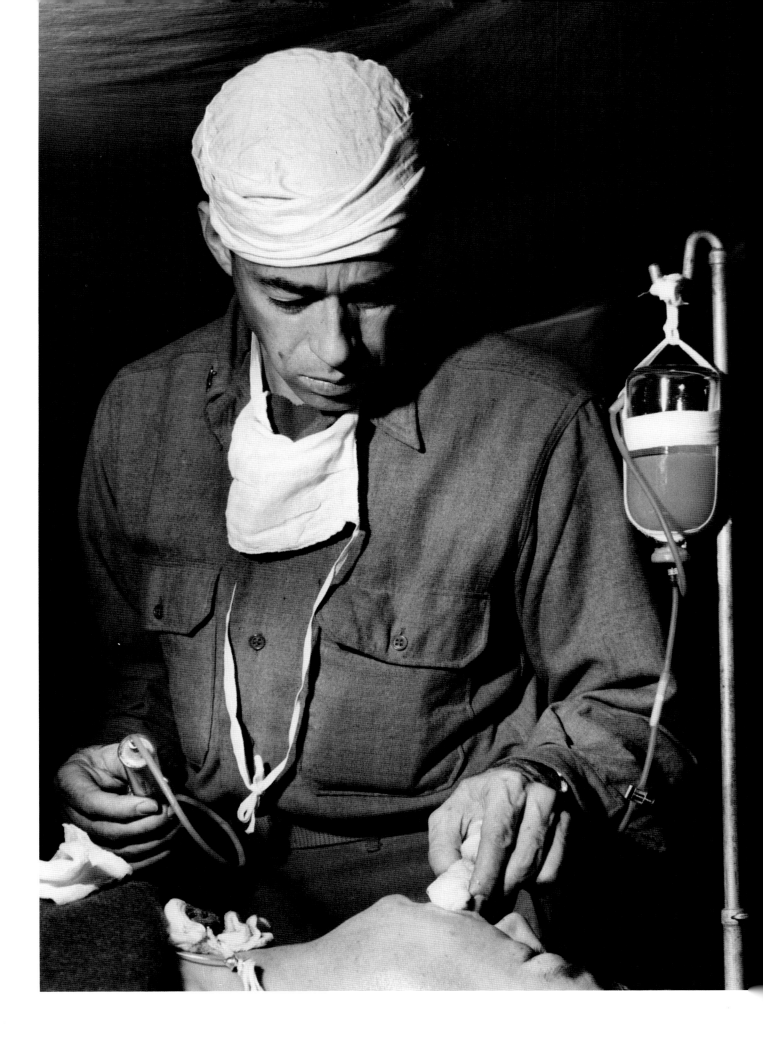

Naples, 1944–45.

Cave dwellers outside Naples, 1944–45.

Naples, 1944–45.

Father and son, Naples, 1944–45.

It was very distressing to Bourke-White that the United States seemed to disdain taking any measures that might help ensure a renewal of democratic values in Italy. She hoped that someone in a position of influence would see that efforts had to be made to erase the pervasive damage fascism had done. Those hopes soon evaporated, however, and Bourke-White's dismay flared into outrage when she finally saw in Germany, in the spring of 1945, that reviving democratic values in Europe was very low on the list of postwar priorities.

Bourke-White took an increasingly dim view of the complacency the United States occupation forces exhibited. In failing to confront the fascist mentality behind Nazi aggression that originally provoked the war, the United States was relinquishing the leadership role the nation had always held in her eyes.

» . . . Germany after the whirlwind had been reaped, was a bottomless pit of malevolence and malignance. Cities and people were broken ruins together, but the venom the Nazis had distilled was virulent yet and held the power to hurt and to poison all men it touched. It touched Americans as well as Germans and it was frightening to see.

It was no accident that the few good people I found were those who stood against tyranny over any other human being, people who had the democratic idea in their hearts. They were so few, so pitiably few. They were not the teachers, as one might hope, not the scientists, not those who had studied in America, not the great industrialists who might be expected to have a world view. No, the men who shared responsibility for the whirlwind, who sat unprotesting as the wind was sown, these men denied responsibility. And we, the victors, were treating them in a way that almost made it seem we didn't believe too deeply in democracy ourselves. «

Everywhere she looked, she saw the horrors of a warped and battered society subsisting on the shreds of its own remains, and that is the vision she comprehensively records in *"Dear Fatherland, Rest Quietly": A Report on the Collapse of Hitler's "Thousand Years."* Flying from Italy via Paris in March 1945, Bourke-White arrived during the last days of fighting around Germany's principal cities, and was frequently one of the first correspondents to follow the conquering Army into newly liberated sites. She toured greater Frankfurt, for example, on the morning after the U.S. infantry had wiped out the last of Hitler's élite SS troops defending the city.

» As we entered the mangled ruin of Greater Frankfurt we had to drive carefully to avoid the twisted figures of the newly fallen dead. But it was the living in the devastated streets that first caught my eyes. Most of them were women, and they were wandering around dazedly with their arms full of flowers. Rising between the skeletons of houses were magnolias and lilacs, filling the incongruous ruins with reminders of spring; and it seemed that these women, climbing up out of the darkness where they had hidden day and night from the terrible shellings, with their first glimpse of daylight were drawn irresistibly to the flowers. It was a sense of return to life that had impelled them to fill their arms with all the pink and purple boughs they could carry.

In the center of the city, under the famous old Rumpelmayer restaurant, a food riot was taking place in the cellar where the crowd had broken into the sugar. At the municipal icehouse quantities of frozen meat had been blown into the street by concussion; after the fighting had ceased, citizens of Frankfurt descended on the meat like maggots. An advance echelon of Military Government had sent guards to food stores to try to prevent looting, and as these MPs' Jeeps swung into the street a hundred Germans dropped quarters of beef before disappearing into the rubble.

We passed a moth-eaten old man who stopped us to explain that the horse he was leading was a military horse, and to inquire where he should take it. He was too dazed to understand that there was no German Army in Frankfurt any longer to lay claim to the horse.

An excited woman was posting a sign on the door of a bookstore, which stated that the premises had been inspected and passed by American Military Government. Actually this was not true, for there had not been time yet for any such procedure; but she was the proprietor, and German property owners were greatly alarmed about American soldiers' looting. Next door was a camera shop, and inside it there was already a group of infantry boys, hacking open wooden packing cases, greatly annoyed to find that they all contained either developing trays and chemicals, or large quantities of optical mirrors for installation in cameras. They had not found one camera in the shop; the proprietor had either hidden his stock somewhere else or carried it with him.

The night before, we learned, the Nazis had put into effect a sweeping evacuation order. Broadcasts told the people that although life might be hard under present conditions, when the Americans came in they would not be able to live at all. American soldiers would rape their daughters. American soldiers sucked blood like vampires. Moreover, Hitler was promising to launch a "counter-death mist," or last-minute offensive. The Gestapo promised to return and punish all who collaborated with the invader. The werewolves would come with fire and sword. Anyone who did not evacuate, it was announced officially, was a traitor.

Thousands of inhabitants risked being called traitors and remained. Some of them, finding their families divided, committed suicide rather than face the loneliness and confusion of the future. But thousands of others, with the traditional obedience of Germans, followed orders and streamed out of the town. This was one of the purposes behind the evacuation order: to choke the roads with people and slow up our tanks. It was noticeable that while the common citizens walked out on foot, the Party officials rode out in private cars, taking all the supplies they could carry with them.

Just before leaving, the Nazis had been swept by a sadistic lust for destruction. They set food stores on fire, threw hand grenades at typewriters, and burned a supply of thousands of cigarettes, rather than give them even to their own people. Even in their haste, they had found time to seek out the archives of the *Frankfurter Zeitung,* records which the editors had hidden away because of the newspaper's anti-Fascist tendencies. Their last act had been to burn these papers. . . . «

Bourke-White saw similar happenings in newly liberated cities all along the western front—Schweinfurt, Leipzig, Cologne, Kassel, Weimar—and the awful trail of destruction and dislocation began to have a dizzying effect. Sergeant Nathan Asch, the famous Yiddish writer Scholem Asch's son, who was Bourke-White's Jeep driver for a period that spring, seemed to sum up the whole situation when he said to Bourke-White one day on the outskirts of Frankfurt: "I can't pick a thread out of this maze of threads. It is still too confused. The picture is blurred."

"I know of no way to convey the feeling of rising violence that we witnessed as we drove deeper into Germany," Bourke-White wrote.

» The waves of suicides, the women throwing themselves after their loved dead into newly dug graves, the passionate denunciations of friends and neighbors, the general lawlessness. Each street corner had its open tragedy; every life seemed shot through with its own individual terror. And over all hung the numbing realization that this newly conquered world was facing a sterile future.

Events were moving too fast to leave time for the considered essays which *Life* customarily featured. No one, neither we on the spot nor *Life*'s hard-pressed editors, could keep up with the furious pace of the news. Never had any of us lived through such a spring. I used to run into our other *Life* photographers, who were as rushed and tormented and baffled as I was. There were eight of us spaced along the western front, which meant we had by far the biggest coverage of any single organization—in fact it was almost as large a total of photographers as that of all the other picture- and news-agencies put together. But all of us, whether photographers or reporters, were painfully aware of the utter impossibility of keeping up with such a torrent of news. We all felt frustrated when we tried to interpret the baffling human kaleidoscope which confronted us. «

One bright April day, shortly after Weimar was captured, Bourke-White found herself facing a vision of ultimate terror at Buchenwald, which she entered with General Patton's Third Army. She saw more ghastliness at the Erla prison camp near Leipzig that same day. Bourke-White devotes a separate chapter of *"Dear Fatherland, Rest Quietly"* to the record of that day's impressions. Although her photographs of the scenes at Buchenwald and Erla are widely known, this is the first time her words have appeared in print in nearly forty years.

» We didn't know! We didn't know!" I first heard these words on a sunny afternoon in mid-April, 1945. They were repeated so often during the weeks to come, and all of us heard them with such monotonous frequency, that we came to regard them as a kind of national chant for Germany.

There was an air of unreality about that April day in Weimar, a feeling to which I found myself stubbornly clinging. I kept telling myself that I would believe the indescribably horrible sight in the courtyard before me only when I had a chance to look at my own photographs. Using the camera was almost a relief; it interposed a slight barrier between myself and the white horror in front of me.

This whiteness had the fragile translucence of snow, and I wished that under the bright April sun which shone from a clean blue sky it would all simply melt away. I longed for it to disappear, because while it was there I was reminded that men actually had done this thing—men with arms and legs and eyes and hearts not so very unlike our own. And it made me ashamed to be a member of the human race.

The several hundred other spectators who filed through the Buchenwald courtyard on that sunny April afternoon were equally unwilling to admit association with the human beings who had perpetrated these horrors. But their reluctance had a certain tinge of self-interest; for these were the citizens of Weimar, eager to plead their ignorance of the outrages.

When 3rd Army troops had occupied Buchenwald two days before, that tough old soldier, General Patton, had been so incensed at what he saw that he ordered his police to go through Weimar, of which Buchenwald is a suburb, and bring back one thousand civilians to make them see with their own eyes what their leaders had done. The MPs were so enraged that they brought back two thousand.

The newly freed inmates of the camp, dressed in their blue and white striped prison suits, scrambled to the top of the fences around the courtyard. From here these slave laborers and political prisoners waited to see German people forced to view the heap of their dead comrades. Women fainted or wept. Men covered their faces and turned their heads away. It was when the civilians began repeating, "We didn't know! We didn't know!" that the ex-prisoners were carried away with wrath.

"You did know," they shouted. "Side by side we worked with you in the factories. At the risk of our lives we told you. But you did nothing."

Of course they knew, as did almost all Germans.

Even during the short time that the two thousand unwilling Germans were in the courtyard, the white pile grew steadily higher. American Army medics, who began feeding the inmates as soon as Buchenwald was captured, were unable to stop the ravages of long suffering and mistreatment. Twelve hundred had died the month before, and people would continue to die there for some time to come. The ironical reason why the pile of naked bodies had been allowed to grow so high, instead of being burned according to regular concentration-camp practice, was that, because of the more pressing needs of the war, Buchenwald had run short of coal.

The presence of many familiar names among the inmates—all correspondents found people in the camp they had known elsewhere, or the relatives of people they had known—served to bring the tragedy closer to reality in our minds. I talked with Eddie Cantor's cousin, a Holland-Dutch Jew, whose circuit of several concentration camps had finally brought him to Buchenwald, where he had spent one year wasting away in Barracks Number 58. But he was one of the lucky ones; he had sufficient physical stamina to react favorably to food and care, and he would live.

Buchenwald was an example of the key part the concentration-camp system played in Germany's industrial scheme. I believe that during the war we vastly underestimated the importance of slave labor in Germany's military resistance. Near Buchenwald was a V-bomb factory where many operations were carried on by forced labor from the concentration camp. Allied Air Force Intelligence knew the location of the prison barracks, which were so close to the factory that our pilots were briefed with especial care to avoid them. During repeated raids on the V-bomb plant, although some bombs inevitably fell close, the camp escaped actual hits for the most part. But although aerial photographs could show the location of Buchenwald, air reconnaissance could furnish no hint of the horrors which ground invasion revealed.

Years before the war the camps existed as what the Germans so appropriately called educational institutions. Their aim in the beginning, so they said, was political: to strangle independent thinking and handle the "race problem." Probably it was with the growing need for armaments under Germany's economy of aggression that their full industrial value was realized, although the German General Staff had included slave labor in its calculations before the Nazis came to power.

We know now that the camps were managed by

personnel who had been given systematic training in cruelty in special schools for their specialized jobs, and that they were run according to a horrible law of diminishing returns. The slave laborers were fed as little as possible and worked until their strength fell below a certain level. Then by various devices—such as the prolonged daily roll call in which the weak ones were made to stand naked in rainy or snowy weather, or by other inexpensive means—the slaves were encouraged to die as fast as possible, in order to save upkeep.

If we had encountered just one camp run by a maniac, we would have considered it merely the work of madness. But at a certain stage in the advance of our armies we began meeting these camps everywhere; along the western front all *Life*'s photographers simultaneously began running into them: Dave Scherman tried to photograph Auschwitz until it made him sick; Florea struck Nordhausen; Vandivert took some unforgettable pictures at Gardelegan near Berlin, and George Rodger made a heart-rending record of Belsen. It was the wide prevalence of the system that testified to its vicious purpose.

A much smaller and less publicized place than those mentioned above brought home to me the full tragedy of the concentration camps. On the afternoon of the same day that Bill Walton and I had canvassed the City Hall, we had driven to the outskirts of Leipzig to hunt up an aircraft small-parts factory which had been an 8th Air Force bombing target. The Leipzig-Mochau plant, in a suburb called Erla, had been one of the units in the Leipzig aircraft complex.

We never found the aircraft factory that afternoon. For a time we became involved in a small pocket where the Germans had surrounded groups of American soldiers who were fighting their way out along the borders—although things were so confused that we did not comprehend the exact status of this area at the time. We did wonder, however, at the shells that were falling uncomfortably close, and were never quite sure whose they were. But soon our preoccupation with even the shelling was lost in a concern about something else. As we searched for the factory along a narrow country road bisecting plowed fields, we began to smell a peculiar odor, quite different from anything in our experience. We followed the smell until we saw, across a small meadow, a ten-foot barbed-wire fence which, curiously, seemed to surround nothing at all. Park-

ing the Jeep, we ran through a small gate into the enclosure, and found ourselves standing at the edge of an acre of bones.

There was no one there; that is, there was no living person. But flying grotesquely over the patch of skulls and charred ribs, from a tall slender flag-pole, was a white surrender flag. There was eloquent testimony that the men who had been there so recently had not willingly surrendered to death. Plunged into the four-foot-wide barrier of closely meshed barbed wire were blackened human figures whose desperate attitudes showed their passionate attempts to break to freedom. Caught in the spiked coils, they had perished, flaming torches, as they tried to escape.

Nothing was left standing among the ashes, except the incongruous flag-pole at the far edge. Dotting the ghastly mottled carpet which covered the area were dozens of identical little graniteware basins and among them a scattering of spoons.

"Look at all the nails on the ground," said Bill. "The building must have gone up so fast that all the nails popped out." Then he sat down on his musette bag on the ground, and put his head in his hands.

Neither of us knew at the time how quickly people at home, and even some returned soldiers who had not seen these things, would begin to say that perhaps accounts had been exaggerated, that maybe the Germans were not so bad after all. But even though I did not realize how soon some people would disbelieve or forget, I had a deep conviction that an atrocity like this demanded to be recorded. So I forced myself to map the place with negatives.

We had been there in silence for almost an hour, I suppose, when an unexpected and moving thing took place. Survivors began drifting back. Bill and I were witness to unbearably pitiful scenes as those few people, coming back from different directions, recognized one another and ran to greet comrades still alive, falling into each other's arms while standing up to their ankles in bones. Among the first to return were a Russian in a peasant sheepskin coat, a Czech wearing the letter T for Tschechoslovakei on his striped prison jacket, and a Pole, who, catching sight of the unburned but hand-grenaded body of a Polish comrade, sank down beside his dead friend, bowed with grief.

When finally eighteen had returned, the survivors decided that these were all who had escaped out of the three hundred whom the Germans had tried to destroy. Originally, we were told, there had been eight hundred, arrested because of political ideas considered impermissible by the Nazis, and confined to the Number Three Erla Work Camp as slave labor for the Leipzig-Mochau aircraft factory. When our armies advanced so close that the Nazi authorities knew Leipzig would soon fall, the Gestapo evacuated five hundred who were still strong enough to be herded on foot to work in another factory deeper in German-held territory. The plan had been to leave the weakest behind. But finally the Gestapo, knowing that political prisoners freed by the Americans were giving whatever useful intelligence they could to our army, decided to annihilate the remaining three hundred.

Bill got the story from the Czech. He was a barber, and to Bill and to me he was the hero of Number Three Erla Work Camp. Having a little more freedom than the others, since he was called upon to shave the SS guards, the barber got wind of the fact that a massacre was planned. The greatest barrier to the chances of escape, he knew, was the 800-volt charge in the barbed-wire fence. He wrote a note which he wrapped around a stone and threw into the inner enclosure at night, warning his comrades of what was afoot, and informing them that he would short-circuit the fence. As soon as the evacuations began taking place, and the camp electrician had been evacuated with certain other staff members, the barber stole out at night, cut the wires, and short-circuited the fence. After throwing in a second note warning the inmates to escape at the first opportunity, he hid at the bottom of a deep bricked hole, coming out only to make sure the wires had not been repaired.

It is surprising how many places there were to hide even in a concentration camp. Some of the inmates managed to dig themselves into holes under the buildings. Unfortunately not enough of them, in their weakened condition, were able to understand the significance of the short-circuited wires, or more might have escaped. They had feared that fence too long.

On the morning that the Americans reached the outskirts of Leipzig, the guards had set out pails of steaming soup to lure the poor hungry wretches conveniently into the mess hall. The soup cans were still recognizable when Bill and I arrived.

After the prisoners were inside, the SS put blankets over the windows, threw in pails of flaming ace-

tate solution, sprinkled the place with machine-gun fire, and tossed in hand grenades. The building must have gone up in a sheet of flame but, even then, many prisoners got as far as the door. We know this because the concentration of skulls were greatest where the door had been. A fair number even broke through the fence. But the Gestapo had previously brought up a couple of tanks manned by Hitler Jugend, and these ferocious youngsters shot down survivors as they ran across the meadow. We could see their bodies where they had fallen in the plowed earth.

Some of the victims were so close to freedom that it made my heart bleed to see them. A Polish professor, who, we were told, had been an aircraft technician, had squeezed halfway through the outer fence. The shriveled lower half of his body lay in cinders within the enclosure, with his charred crutch close by, but the fine intellectual bald head thrust through to the outside was still unmarred, with even the spectacles in place. He must have been much loved; the survivors shed many tears over him. Another half-intact figure had a silver cross hanging around his neck. The dead body was covered with blisters. The Czech knelt down, gently touched the crucifix, and said, "Blood on the cross."

The barber started hunting through each hole and dugout, hoping against hope to find someone alive. Suddenly he jumped into a trench and, raising his clenched fist, cried, "My comrade. A Czech." In the dim light at the entrance to the little underground tunnel I could just make out the face of his friend, the fine features streaked with blood. The Gestapo had evidently hunted out all who hid in holes, and machine-gunned them.

Then the barber began searching for some remembrance which he could carry back to the family of his friend. There was little to choose from, and finally he took the only thing he could find to carry away. What he did will sound strange—perhaps grotesque—when I describe it from so far away. But against this background I felt I was watching one of those rare acts prompted by deep inner sympathy. The man lifted out his comrade's false teeth, and, looking up at me, said simply: "For the wife of my friend."

I thought that I had seldom heard more moving words. «

With the termination of the war in Europe in the spring of 1945, Bourke-White herself came to the end of an assignment which had extended back as far as 1932, the year she photographed Germany's Reichswehr rearming. She had photographed part of the prologue to war in the Sudetenland in 1938; seen how events were unfolding with the first extension of the war into the world at large in England and the Mideast in 1939–1940; recorded the first explosions at the Russian Front in 1941; soared in a United States bomber in 1942; walked in the mud with her country's troops in Italy in 1943–1944; and witnessed Germany in defeat at last in 1945.

The scenes that passed before her lenses were constantly changing, but her writing reveals that she always sought the same currents in the nearly unbroken stream of history that composed her experiences for the duration of the war.

Her concern for the issues behind the surface of the news was consistent; in fact, her perspective grew very broad, and above all her powers of insight and understanding matured. Yet, despite the probing critical eye with which she viewed the conduct of war, Bourke-White's thinking never turned into cynicism.

She knew that fascism had not been conquered. But she maintained hope that democracy would ultimately prevail.

» We turned our backs on our greatest opportunity to do something constructive with the youth of Germany. We had no plan, no desire, no willingness, it seemed, to teach a democratic way of life. We poured out lives and boundless treasure to win a mechanical victory and now we had no patience for the things of the spirit which alone can save us from another far greater catastrophe. It was time to go home.

The driver of a staff car told me, with bitterness, of two congressmen whom he had driven when they visited Berlin. They asked to be taken at once to the black market, even before going to their billets. As soon as they saw the crowd they whipped open their suitcases. One sold a blue pinstripe suit for $500. The other had an extra pair of trousers with his gray herringbone tweed. He got $600.

I could not blame the boys who wanted to go home with their pitiful pocketings of black market money. They had the best examples. I could only blame Americans for understanding too little, for taking part too little in the affairs of a world now shrunken to our doorstep. We had let our boys go off to war with so little comprehension of what the fight was for. Men who are ordered to put their lives in hazard should be asked to take this risk only for the highest purposes. They deserve to know what these purposes are, and to know they will be fulfilled after the victory.

We did not bring democracy to Germany, although we talked a lot about it. Even now it is not too late, because democracy isn't something a nation tools up for: it lives in its citizens, in the way they live with their fellow men. We can make up for time lost and wasted and we can give to the Germans, and to others as well, some things more than techniques. Unless we do, this war will be without meaning for us, and some of the hope for a good world will die down in the hearts of men everywhere. «

———

Shopping center of Cologne after bombardment, 1945.

German bunker outside Würzburg, 1945.

Field Marshal Hermann Wilhelm Göring after his surrender in 1945

General George S. Patton, Luxembourg, 1945.

Survivors, Frankfurt, 1945.

Suicides, Leipzig, 1945.

Buchenwald, 1945.

Citizens of Weimar view Buchenwald, 1945.

Erla death camp, 1945.

Buchenwald, 1945.

Erla, 1945.

Bourke-White toured in Germany for *Life* until the conclusion of the war, but stayed until October 1945, learning as much as she could about postwar Germany in order to write *"Dear Fatherland, Rest Quietly."* It was published in the fall of 1946, when she returned from her first trip to India, where *Life* had sent her on assignment in the spring of that year.

"I had always thought of India as an old country," Bourke-White wrote in *Portrait of Myself*. "It was a discovery to learn she was also a very young one. My insatiable desire to be on the scene when history is being made was never more nearly fulfilled. I arrived . . . when India stood shining and full of hope on the threshold of independence."

The gleaming personality behind India's struggle for independence from British rule was Mahatma Gandhi, whose original methods of nonviolent resistance have continued to be effective weapons in the fight against injustice. Because *Life* had scheduled a feature on India's political leaders, Bourke-White's India assignment began almost immediately with photographing Gandhi.

She had made an appointment for a portrait session through Gandhi's secretary, Pyarelal. But when the appointed time came, Pyarelal told Bourke-White that if she wanted to see Gandhi, she would first have to learn how to use the *charka*, or spinning wheel, which she was told typified what Gandhi had called "the proletarianism of science."

"Consider the great machines of the factories, with all their complex mechanisms, and consider the charka," Pyarelal told Bourke-White. "The hand-driven spinning wheel reached the highest coefficient of efficiency," he went on. "And I will give you another tip," Pyarelal said. "While your camera will cover the outward appearance of Gandhiji, your story on spinning will interpret his soul. Therefore, you must first systematically master the principles of the *charka*."

Pyarelal offered to give Bourke-White spinning lessons the following Tuesday, but Bourke-White could not wait because her films had to be air-couriered back to *Life*'s offices in New York within forty-eight hours to meet the deadline for the next issue.

"I do not remember exactly how I persuaded Gandhi's secretary that I must have my spinning lesson today—this very day. And that the appointment with the Mahatma must follow. My methods were nonviolent—but just barely!" Bourke-White wrote in 1949.

Of her first lesson in spinning Bourke-White wrote: "It did not help my opinion of my own IQ to see how often and how awkwardly I broke the thread. I began to appreciate as never before the machine age, with its ball bearings and steel parts, and maybe an occasional nail to take over from the human hand."

In later years, however, Bourke-White saw the incident of the spinning wheel in a different light. She observed in *Portrait of Myself*:

» Translated into the many situations a photographer must meet, the rule set up by Gandhi's secretary was a good one: if you want to photograph a man spinning, give some thought to why he spins. Understanding, for a photographer, is as important as the equipment he uses. I have always believed what goes on, unseen, in back of the lens is just as important as what goes on in front of it. In the case of Gandhi, the spinning wheel was laden with meaning. For millions of Indians, it was the symbol of the fight for freedom. Gandhi was a shrewd judge of economic pressures as well as spiritual ones. If millions of Indians could be persuaded to make the cloth they used themselves, instead of buying manufactured textiles from the British colonial power, the boycott would be severely felt in England's textile industry. The charka was the key to victory. Nonviolence was Gandhi's creed, and the spinning wheel was the perfect weapon. «

For years Gandhi had guided the people of India on a nonviolent path to independence, and in the spring of 1946, with British-Indian freedom negotiations occurring in New Delhi, the Gandhian revolution was on the verge of achieving its long-awaited goal. But with freedom on the horizon, Mohammed Ali Jinnah, head of India's Muslim League, who had worked with Nehru and the Hindu-dominated Congress Party for a free, united India, broke sharply with his past and launched his own campaign to form a separate state, Pakistan.

Jinnah had been conspicuously absent from the freedom talks in New Delhi. The suspense was keen, therefore, when in late July 1946 Jinnah announced that he would hold a press conference. At the press conference, held in Jinnah's fashionable Bombay home, the Muslim League leader announced that the Muslims were forced for their own self-protection to abandon constitutional methods. "The decision we have taken is a very grave one," Bourke-White heard Jinnah say. If the Muslims were not granted their separate Pakistan they would launch "direct action." Finally, Jinnah challenged the Congress Party, declaring: "If you want peace, we do not want war. If you want war we accept your offer unhesitatingly. We will either have a divided India or a destroyed India."

On August 16, 1946, the day Jinnah had proclaimed as "Direct Action Day," violence broke out in Calcutta. Bourke-White flew to Calcutta from Bombay as soon as she heard of the incredible events taking place. She made her way to the ruined heart of Calcutta's bazaar and hunted for an eyewitness. She found Nanda Lal in the wreckage of his teashop.

» Nanda Lal's little "East Bengal Cabin," at 36 Harrison Road, was located in one of those potential trouble spots where a by-lane of Muslim shops crossed the Hindu-dominated thoroughfare. Nanda Lal was a Hindu and wore the traditional dhoti, twisted diaperlike between his legs. A patch of grizzled hair stood out on his walnut-colored chest, and a narrow silver amulet gleamed on his thin upper arm. Like many Bengalis, he was fairly well educated and spoke a little English.

The East Bengal Cabin, with its elongated oven fronting the sidewalk, looked much like an Asiatic version of a Nedick's stand. The Hindu clerks of the Minerva Banking Corporation across the street were frequent customers, as were the boarders in the "Happy Home Boarding House" near by. Although Nanda Lal was in the protective shadow of these impressive Hindu establishments, the Muslim quarter began just around the corner on Mirzapore Street, too close for security.

On the morning of August 16th, Nanda Lal started his oven and set out his tray of sweetmeats as usual. When his little son came out with jars of mango pickle and chutney, he commented to the child that the streets looked reassuringly quiet. The sacred cows that roam freely through the thoroughfares of Calcutta were sleeping as usual in the middle of the car tracks, and rose to their feet reluctantly, as they always did, when the first streetcar of the day clanged down Harrison Road.

It was the sight of the first tram that confirmed Nanda Lal's fears that this day was to be unlike all

Practicing spinning, India, 1946.

other days. Normally it was so crowded with commuters that they bulged from the platform and clung to the doorsteps and back of the car. Today there was hardly a passenger on board.

Then things began happening so quickly that Nanda Lal could hardly recall them in sequence. But he did remember quite clearly the seven lorries that came thundering down Harrison Road. Men armed with brickbats and bottles began leaping out of the lorries—Muslim "goondas," or gangsters, Nanda Lal decided, since they immediately fell to tearing up Hindu shops. Some rushed into the furniture store next to the Happy Home and began tossing mattresses and furniture into the street. Others ran toward the Bengal Cabin, but Nanda Lal was fastening up the blinds by now, shouting to his son to run back into the house, straining to bar the windows and close the door.

He could hear a pelting sound beating up the street, the hammering noise of a hail of stones. He was too busy getting the windows barred to take much notice of the fact that he was hit in several places and his leg and head were bleeding. He managed to get inside by the time the ruffians reached his

With Dwight D. Eisenhower at Rutgers University, where she received an honorary degree, 1948.

shop; he could hear them banging against his door as he double-barred it from the inside; then he raced across the inner courtyard.

The court was edged with tenements and closed from the outside by a wall. Nanda Lal could hear goondas climbing the wall, shouting: "Beat them up! Beat them up!" A head rose over the wall, and then several figures started pulling themselves up into view. But by that time some of Nanda Lal's numerous relatives, who lived in his flat, had taken up a counter-offensive from the terrace and the invaders were driven back under a shower of flower pots.

In the breathing spell offered by this successful move, two of his wife's uncles ran down and helped Nanda Lal build a barricade at the foot of the stairs which would jam shut the door leading to their flat. Whatever benches and tables they could lay their hands on, they piled against the door and at the foot of the stairs. Nanda Lal snatched three bicycles from

the vestibule and jammed them in amidst the furniture. Then they all ran up to the top floor of the flat, where the women of the house were huddled in the upper hallway.

Nanda Lal peeped cautiously out of a window. Never had he seen the streets so filled with clawing, surging mobs. . . . The streets and by-lanes were throbbing with cries of "*Jai Hind.* Victory to a united India" from the Hindus, and "*Pakistan zindabad.* Long live Pakistan" from the Muslims. Suddenly this clash of slogans was punctuated by a new staccato sound. A rattle of bullets from the window of an apartment opposite the college brought cold terror to the heart of Nanda Lal. Gunfire is rare in Indian riots. A new frenzy swept the throng and the riot overflowed the bounds of Harrison Road. Through the entire city the terror and arson spread, through the crowded bazaars, the teeming chawls and tenements.

During the terrible days that followed, Nanda Lal huddled with his family and relatives in the upper hallway. Sometimes bricks and stones crashed through the windows of the outside rooms. The children cried a great deal; they were hungry as well as terrified. . . .

On the fourth day Nanda Lal noted that the weapons in the street fighting had grown heavier. Soda-water bottles had given way to iron staves, and unfortunately the neighborhood had a plentiful supply of rails from the fence surrounding the near-by Shraddhananda Park. Finally, as the skirmish of the iron pikes reached its fiercest, a convoy of three military tanks rolled through and machine-gunned the mobs, and along with them the police made their belated appearance.

The police, I learned later, had refused to come out without military escort, fearing they might become the target of the fighting. Many times, as "faithful servants of the British Empire," the police had been ordered to fire on their own people, both Hindu and Muslim, at freedom demonstrations, and now they feared the anger of their aroused countrymen. When the militia was at last ordered out— and when Muslim and Hindu leaders finally put aside their own differences and made joint appeals—the riots began dying down.

When peace returned to Calcutta on the fifth day, the streets were a rubble of broken bricks and broken bottles, bloated remains of cows, and charred wrecks of automobiles and victorias rising above the strewn figures of the dead. The human toll had reached six thousand according to official count, and sixteen thousand according to unofficial sources. In this great city, as large as Detroit, vast areas were dark with ruin and black with the wings of vultures that hovered impartially over the Hindu and Muslim dead.

Thousands began fleeing Calcutta. For days the bridge over the Hooghly River, one of the longest steel spans in the world, was a one-way current of men, women, children, and domestic animals, headed toward the Howrah railroad station. . . .

But fast as the refugees fled, they could not keep ahead of the swiftly spreading tide of disaster. Calcutta was only the beginning of a chain reaction of riot, counter-riot, and reprisal which stormed through India for an entire year. . . .

Months of violence sharpened the divisions, highlighted Jinnah's arguments, achieved partition. On August 15, 1947, exactly one day less than a year after Nanda Lal had seen direct action break out on his doorstep, a bleeding Pakistan was carved out of the body of a bleeding India. «

Bourke-White returned to the United States in October 1946, began assembling her pictures and her impressions, and, as she had become accustomed to doing after a big trip, started writing a book.

"Trying to understand this complex country so I could make it clear to others called out everything I had to give," Bourke-White recalled in *Portrait of Myself.* But although she generally found that writing a book became easier as she progressed, her book on India was not following the same course. "I wrote half a book. Then, all at once, I saw what the trouble was. I just did not know enough to write a book about India, and I arranged to send myself back."

Just prior to her second departure for India, in September 1947, religious violence in India and Pakistan again broke out. *Life* commissioned her to do a story on the great exchange of populations and the new nation of Pakistan, and at the last moment CBS engaged Bourke-White to do some live radio broadcasts. The network had never been able to set up proper radio reception from India, and Bourke-White was to try.

A massive shift was under way in the Punjab area, in the north of India, when Bourke-White arrived there in the fall of 1947. Five million people were on the move. "They flowed in a two-way stream across the border," Bourke-White wrote in *Halfway to Freedom.*

» Into the Indian Union came the Hindus and Sikhs (differing slightly in their religious practices, the warlike Sikhs, famous for their picturesque beards and turbans, are an offshoot of the Hindu religion; the Muslims poured into their new Pakistan, which they looked on as their Promised Land. All were led by fear, by highly questionable leadership, by ever-dwindling hope. What had been merely arbitrarily drawn areas on a map began emptying and refilling with human beings— neatly separated into so-called "opposite" religious communities—as children's crayons fill in an outline map in geography class. But this was no child's play. This was a massive exercise in human misery. . . .

Babies were born along the way. People died along the way. Some died of cholera, some from the attacks of hostile religious communities. But many of them simply dropped out of line from sheer weariness, and sat by the roadside to wait patiently for death. Sometimes, I saw children pulling at the arms and hands of a parent or grandparents, unable to comprehend that those arms would never be able to carry them again. The name "Pakistan" means Land of the Pure: many of the pure never got there. The way to their Promised Land was lined with graves. «

Four million Hindus and Sikhs were leaving Pakistan. "But with six million Muslims coming in," Bourke-White wrote, "this infant land of the Pure seemed in danger of being swept away by the very numbers of the pure pouring into it."

» This basic Sikh religious principle, worshiping one God as the Muslims do, instead of a whole hierarchy of gods (along with trees, rivers, and the sacred cow) as do other Hindus, made it seem unreasonable that Sikhs and Muslims should be at each other's throats in the religious bloodshed which was sweeping India. This was only one of many things which were to make me wonder increasingly whether the "religious wars" were really religious at all, or whether they weren't being used as a cloak for something else. And later I was to learn more about the practical uses of these so-called religious differences. . . .

Since the time of my first arrival in India a year and a half before Independence Day, I had watched the constant jockeying for position which had finally resulted in the creation not of a single free, united nation, but of these handicapped twins. I remember the many times when bloodshed had broken out during the preliminary sparring and the Pakistan promoters had said, "We must have our separate nation, or we will not have peace." But now that this separate nation had become a reality the people had not achieved peace. It was a little too soon to find out just what they had achieved.

"Whoever thought Pakistan would mean this to a Musselman!" one of the weary pilgrims said to me as he trudged toward his Promised Land.

"We were promised a Sikhistan," said the Sikhs, as they journeyed from the land to which they had given so much, "but now we no longer expect to see happy days." And one of them, whom I shall always remember for the great dignity of his bearing in spite of the dust which caked his turban and patriarchal beard, added a moving thought: "For the Musselmans too the future is dark. They are helpless just like us. They have been rendered homeless just as we have been. They are the victims of the same fate." **«**

———

The noble Sikh could not have been more correct with regard to the fate of India's Muslims. An enormous minority of forty million Muslims lived within India's borders. Many of them had opposed partition and wanted to continue to live and work in a united India.

"With the great flight of Hindus and Sikhs from their old homes in Pakistan," Bourke-White wrote, "tens of thousands of these refugees had crowded into Delhi, only to find that there was no shelter for them. Having lost their farms and houses to hostile Muslims in Pakistan, they had begun taking forcible possession of the houses of Muslims. The Delhi police, who were largely Sikh and Hindu and therefore partisan, stood by passively and watched Muslims being evicted, looted, and murdered. When Hindu and Sikh refugees began storming into Muslim mosques, and sacred tombs, Gandhi felt that action must be taken."

Contrasting with Jinnah's "direct action," the action Gandhi decided to take strictly conformed to the nonviolent tradition he had followed throughout the struggle for independence. To calm the whirlwind of religious bloodshed that partition had unloosed, Gandhi resolved to begin fasting.

The fast was announced on Monday, January 12, 1948. "This would be the sixteenth fast of Gandhi's life," Bourke-White wrote. "It was more of a bombshell than the previous fifteen had been. The others had been directed against the British Raj, but this was a hunger strike against the omissions of the new free government which Gandhi himself had done so much to create."

Bourke-White was broadcasting to America on the day Gandhi began his fast, and recognizing how difficult it would be to convey to Americans the significance of a Gandhi fast she sought out Jawaharlal Nehru, who generously provided the insight Bourke-White needed.

"Voluntary suffering has great effect on the Indian mind," Nehru explained, emphasizing the word "voluntary." "Gandhi is a kind of sentinel who stands apart. He has felt great distress at the barriers growing up in India. He felt he must take the final step to direct people's minds, to divert them from wrong paths. The fast does two things. It introduces a sense of urgency to the problem and forces people to think out of the ruts—to think afresh. It produces a favorable psychological atmosphere. Then it is up to others to take advantage of this atmosphere."

Bourke-White was present at the first evening prayer meeting Gandhi held following the start of his fast and heard the Mahatma say: "Hindus and Sikhs and Muslims must live as brothers here. Unless we examine the whole situation and search our hearts and stop these things that have been happening, there is no hope for us. Hindus and Sikhs must see that there is no retaliation, whatever Muslims elsewhere may do. Some say I am fasting only for Muslims. That is true only in part, I fast to purify myself."

Gandhi's words had a poignant effect on Bourke-White:

» This is really it, I thought. He has himself on trial. He has a religious position of his own to defend. . . . His whole philosophy of nonviolence is at stake. He cannot accept this chaos which has swept India. He could not survive another Calcutta carnage, another Punjab. He is afraid

With Edward Steichen, 1961. Photograph by Bob Henriques.

everything he stands for in the eyes of the world may prove a myth.

It was plain that Gandhi was launching the hardest battle of his life: the battle to conquer inner hatreds. For thirty years he had fought an outside power and with his weapon of nonviolence had been spectacularly successful in leading the people along the road to freedom. Now he was faced with a still more difficult job: the task of winning tolerance and unity within men's hearts. As he talked on in his quiet voice I had the feeling that he possessed a real power to call on those people's inner strength, for, I thought, he is closer to the soul of India than any other man. **«**

The immediate effects of Gandhi's fast were inconsequential. But each day the crowds at the evening prayer meetings grew bigger. Public support was building for the unity Gandhi had laid his life on the line to achieve. Then, on the fifth day of the fast, Nehru spoke at the evening prayer gathering. Nehru's words had often focused public opinion; his appearance on this occasion, Bourke-White knew, could signal the turning point of the conflict. She could not afford to miss one word.

"I wanted a good translator when I listened to Nehru," Bourke-White wrote, "because Nehru, an artist in his use of both Hindustani and English, was sure to speak to this crowd in their native tongue."

» Looking around for someone I knew, I spotted Bedi and Chari. Bedi was always easy to pick out—he towered above any crowd—and under the protection of this man-mountain I managed to get to the foot of the garden pavilion. Pandit Nehru had mounted the little prayer platform and was speaking into the microphone, requesting people to sit down and be as quiet as possible so as not to disturb the Mahatma. Bedi took the great oatmeal blanket off his shoulders, spread it on the ground, and we sat down on it as Panditji began his impromptu talk to his people.

"I saw the freedom of India as a vision. I had charted the future of Asia on my heart." Bedi whispered his translation, as Nehru spoke of their high aspirations, how they had reached out toward them even as a slave nation. "We felt that India would be a great free country in this disturbed world. It was the aspiration of our youth. It was our pride. In the final analysis, countries do not attain freedom only on maps. The sentiment of freedom surges from the hearts."

As Nehru talked, I found his words were helping me to read a deeper meaning into the long fight for independence "on the map" and for progress and extended freedom as well. "No outside power could free India," Nehru was saying. After having talked with hundreds of people during my nearly two years' stay in India, I had no doubt that it was a mistaken notion to think of independence as a voluntary offering from the British Empire to the Indians. Each concession, each gain toward self-government, had come only after struggle and sacrifice. From the mass movements following the first World War, through the countless arrests and soul-wasting years in prison (in which Nehru had so fully shared), each rung in the ladder had been hammered into place, until the revolt within the ranks of the Royal Indian Navy spectacularly heralded the finish of the fight. With Britain's own armed forces in India streaming off their ships to join hands with the people in the streets in the clamor for freedom, it was plain that there was no longer any choice except withdrawal for the British Raj. But however equitably and gracefully the British tried to withdraw, the divide-and-rule policy was left as a heritage; now self-rule had come but division remained. And because the bitterness must be somehow cleaned away before India could realize the fruits of freedom, a beloved old man, growing weaker by the hour, was making his last and greatest fight for unity.

"Thirty years ago Gandhiji arrived on the scene," Nehru was saying. "An odd-looking man. No art of dressing and no polish in his ways of speech. He did not indulge in high politics. He only said, 'Follow truth. If our goal is good, the path to it should also be righteous. If we want to be free, we must free each other first. Only a free people can lay the foundations of a free land.' These were the lessons of Gandhiji. He had warned us, if we swerve from the path of righteous behavior, we shall be ruined."

Nehru's slight figure had dwindled to a mere blur, as his voice came out of the darkness. And then something very beautiful happened in the garden. Someone who had just pushed his way in with his bicycle shone the lamp on the handlebars across the heads of the seated people toward Nehru. Then more and more cyclists turned their lamps on him, until the whole garden seemed to be flickering with fireflies. When someone with a lamp squeezed his way in near us, Bedi took my notebook and began writing in its light, taking down Nehru's words in swift, hook-shaped Urdu characters, dashing off English phrases for me between his lines of Indian script.

"I am not a religious man," Bedi translated Nehru's words, "but I do believe at moments that we pay for our past deeds. It is those acts which determine our future. I believe, be it a nation or a country, it cannot escape the fruits of what it sows in the fields of its deeds." (I shall always treasure this notebook for those beautiful words, inscribed in decorative characters.) "We are surrounded by sorrow, even though we achieved freedom. Again and again thoughts come to my mind. What ill deeds are we paying for?"

Jawaharlal Nehru had cherished a plan in the past for an Asian federation, following the spiritual leadership of India, and I was greatly interested that he referred to it here in his impromptu garden talk. He spoke of his dream of the new India—its place in Asia—"and through Asia of our role in the world. These visions of mine have not been effaced, even today. Only sometimes fear grips my mind whether, in the short span of life left in front of us, we have got time enough to realize our dreams in reality.

"It is a sustaining thought in moments of heartbreaking despair that after all there is something great and vital in the soil of our country which can produce a Gandhi, a personality of his character, even though a Gandhi may be born only after a thousand years. Let us take the cue to our actions from the guidance which he gives with over seventy years of wisdom at the back of him. He will lead us to the true goal and not to the false dawn of our hopes. . . ." «

Bourke-White had supper with Nehru at his home after the prayer gathering. As she was leaving, a Congress Party official arrived, deeply concerned about Gandhi's condition. "Another twenty-four hours, and it may be too late."

» Early the next morning I went to Birla House and waited all morning outside the door with the anxious crowd. It was a few minutes past noon when a happy cry of women's voices sounded from inside the house. I picked up my camera and ran inside, and in a moment I was with Sushila and the grandnieces and a tight-packed group of men and women in Gandhi's room, and everybody was laughing and crying for joy. Gandhiji was going to break his fast. A peace program had been drawn up and signed in his presence by an astonishing range of Sikh and Hindu leaders representing shades of religious opinion that had never approached agreement before. The delegates fanned from the moderates to the fanatics. At the extremist end of the scale, the signers included that militant champion of Hindu supremacy, the Hindu Mahasabha, and its Sikh counterpart, the equally militant and orthodox Akali Shahidi Jatha. The seldom-seen and almost mythical president of the R.S.S. had come in person that morning to affix his signature. Either Gandhiji has truly worked a miracle, I thought when I heard this, or the Youth Movement leader has his tongue in his cheek. A phrase of the secret R.S.S. creed was still fresh in my mind: "to abolish Islam root and branch."

The High Commissioner of Pakistan had also come in person, and from Pakistan as well as India Gandhi had received what his happy followers referred to as "a spate of telegrams." These telegrams overflowed the desk, the tables, and the window sills, and Gandhiji, where he lay smiling on his mattress in a corner of the floor, was clutching a telegram in his long thin hand.

I jumped on the desk and got my camera into action. Pretty little Abbha burst in with a tall glass of fruit juice, knelt beside Gandhi, and he kissed her. But before he would take even a sip of orange juice he asked for a microphone. A general to his people, as always, he announced his decision to the waiting crowds outside in a faint voice hoarse with exhaustion. Only then did he accept the fruit juice, which the Muslim Cabinet Minister Maulana Azad and Pandit Nehru made a little ceremony of handing him alternately.

Then the women followers flocked in carrying trays of orange slices which Gandhi blessed. This was

prasad, God's gift. The women passed the fruit platters to the crowd, and people, sobbing with happiness, eagerly reached for the orange slices, sharing them with one another and even passing bits of orange up to me where I stood taking pictures on the tabletop, so that a foreigner, too, could share in God's gift.

The whole nation seemed to have shared God's gift. Gandhiji's fast had stirred up a fount of emotion and great soul-searching. Although sporadic outbreaks continued to occur, especially in explosive border areas or where the greatest refugee concentrations showed only too bitterly that problems remained unsolved, Gandhiji's heroic risking of his life had wrought profound effects. The entire country had been stirred to its foundations, and the people bent their will toward peace. . . .

But the militant youths of the R.S.S., its numbers swelled by young refugees who could find no constructive outlets in their uprooted lives, continued to meet for their morning milk and exercises and continued to warm their adolescent imaginations over the glories of the pure Hinduism of two thousand years ago. «

On January 30, 1948, the day before her scheduled departure from India, Bourke-White had one final encounter with Gandhi, which was to be the last encounter with a journalist Gandhi would ever have. Only a few hours after answering Bourke-White's questions, Gandhi was assassinated by Nathuram Vinayak Godse, a member of the R.S.S., the fanatic Hindu youth group devoted to the annihilation of all Muslims.

It had taken two years for Bourke-White to come to grips with India; and only in the last two weeks of her stay there had she begun to understand Gandhi.

"As Nehru expressed it," Bourke-White wrote, " 'in a dissolving world he has been like a rock of purpose and a lighthouse of truth.' On our own side of the globe, our world seemed in danger of dissolving, and I felt this steady voice might have something to say to us."

After obtaining answers to many of the questions Bourke-White had wanted to ask Gandhi, she began speaking of "the weight with which our new and terrible atomic knowledge hangs over us, and of our increasing fear of atomic war. Holding in our uncertain hands the key to the ultimate in violence, we might draw some guidance, I hoped, from the apostle of nonviolence."

» I asked Gandhi whether he believed America should stop manufacturing the atom bomb. Unhesitatingly he replied, "Of course, America should stop."

We went on to talk of this, Gandhi speaking thoughtfully, sometimes haltingly, always with most profound sincerity, I jotting down his words, and neither of us could know that this was to be one of the last—perhaps his very last—message to the world.

Since this momentous day, many people have asked me whether one knew when in Gandhi's presence that there was an extraordinary man. The answer is yes. One knew! And never had I felt it more strongly than on this day, when the inconsistencies that had so troubled me dropped away and Gandhi began to reach forward and probe into that dreadful problem which has overwhelmed all of us. Nehru has said of Gandhi that he was "obviously not of the world's ordinary coinage; he was minted of a different and rare variety," and during these last moments of our talk I felt, as Nehru has expressed it, that sometimes "the unknown stared at us through his eyes."

I had asked Gandhiji how he would meet the atom bomb. Would he meet it with nonviolence?

"Ah, ah!" he said. "How shall I answer that!" The charkha turned busily in his agile hands for a moment, and then he replied: "I would meet it by prayerful action." He emphasized the word "action," and I asked what form it would take.

"I will not go underground. I will not go into shelters. I will come out in the open and let the pilot see I have not the face of evil against him."

He turned back to his spinning for a moment before continuing.

"The pilot will not see our faces from his great height, I know. But that longing in our hearts that he will not come to harm would reach up to him and his eyes would be opened. Of those thousands who were done to death in Hiroshima, if they had died with that prayerful action—died openly with that prayer in their hearts—then the war would not have ended so disgracefully as it has. It is a question now whether the victors are really victors or victims"—he was speaking very slowly and his words had become

toneless and low—"of our own lust . . . and omission. Because the world is not at peace"—his voice had sunk almost to a whisper—"it is still more dreadful. . . ."

My time was up now, and I rose to leave. I folded my hands together in a *namaskar*—the gesture of greeting and farewell which Indians use instead of shaking hands. But Gandhiji held out his hand to me, and shook hands cordially in Western fashion. We said good-by, and I started off.

Then something made me turn back. Perhaps it was because his manner had been so friendly. I stopped, looked over my shoulder, and said, "Good-by—and good luck."

Only a few hours later this man who believed that even the atom bomb should be met with nonviolence was struck down by revolver bullets. And from those who were at his side in that dark moment we know that as he fell his hands were raised in prayer, and the word "Ram"—meaning "God"—was on his lips. «

———

Mahatma Gandhi, 1946.

Jawaharlal Nehru, 1946.

Mohammed Ali Jinnah, 1947.

Refugee camp, New Delhi, 1947.

Refugees, India, 1947.

India, 1947.

Mahatma Gandhi with his granddaughter and grandniece, 1947.

Mourners at Gandhi's funeral pyre, 1948.

Margaret Bourke-White was forty-six years old at the midpoint of the twentieth century, and her career was in full and triumphant bloom. The Boston Chamber of Commerce presented her with the American Woman of Achievement Citation in 1951: "In recognition of her notable achievement in her chosen field of endeavor and her great contribution to American Womanhood." That same year, Bourke-White also received an honorary doctorate of fine arts degree from the University of Michigan. That was, in fact, her second honorary doctorate. Rutgers University had awarded Bourke-White an honorary doctorate of letters degree on June 9, 1948, on which occasion, Dwight David Eisenhower also received an honorary doctorate from Rutgers. There were other citations, awards, and honors. Margaret Bourke-White had become one of the eminent personalities of postwar America.

Halfway to Freedom: A Report on the New India, the last of Bourke-White's books to comprise a careful examination of a chapter in world history, was published in the fall of 1949. Bourke-White continued to lecture and occasionally wrote newspaper and magazine articles, but did not publish a book again until 1963, when *Portrait of Myself* came out.

She began work on *Portrait of Myself* in 1955. Under normal circumstances the book would have taken a seasoned writer like Bourke-White far less than seven years to complete. But for the first time in her life she was working under a serious and constantly worsening handicap. In 1953 she contracted Parkinson's disease, and although she fought it with every ounce of strength she had, Margaret Bourke-White died of Parkinson's on August 27, 1971.

"Parkinsonism is a strange malady," Bourke-White wrote in *Portrait of Myself*. "It works its way into all paths of life, into all that is graceful and human and outgiving in our lives, and poisons it all." Indeed, it had done a cruel job on Bourke-White. Her ability to move and hold things steadily was increasingly impaired. By constant exercise she could forestall the paralysis of her arms, legs, and hands; she was ordered to walk four miles a day and to crumple paper balls constantly. Still, the prognosis in the mid-fifties for Parkinson's disease was devastating: there was no cure.

Late in 1958, however, Bourke-White found one last hope. Dr. Irving S. Cooper had developed a surgical technique that produced dramatic improvements in the symptoms of Parkinsonism. "Like all great things," Bourke-White wrote in *Portrait of Myself*, "his procedure was simple. He drilled a hole in the skull the size of a dime. Checking everything on X-rays as he worked, he probed for precisely that spot which was responsible for the patient's difficulties. The more conservative members of the medical world were skeptical. Gaining recognition was an uphill road for him."

Dr. Cooper operated on Bourke-White's right cranial area in January 1959. Following the operation, she experienced a definite improvement in the rigidity of her left side. Two years later Dr. Cooper operated on the left side of Bourke-White's brain.

A few weeks following the second operation Bourke-White wrote to her regular physician: "I am glad to report to you that we had wonderful success with the operation. Dr. Cooper did a magnificent job. He was very pleased and so was I. Both my hands are completely free of any kind of tremor. My right hand has come back stronger than the left and is taking the lead as the right hand should. With walking, I just sail along and ever so many things have become easier to do. Except for a slight lean to the left and a little difficulty turning up the toe of the right foot, there is little that can be criticized, and these things can be exercised out. I am, however, having some trouble with speech but it is clearing up quite fast with speech therapy and I feel sure I can overcome it very soon. I am continuing my exercise regime even more strongly than before because I think it it so important in these weeks to build good habits."

One month later Bourke-White reported again to her regular physician: "I am in simply wonderful shape, both my hands, feet and entire body as far as I can tell do everything perfectly well, and I think the operation was an outstanding success. The only real difficulty I am having is with my speech and that has already grown stronger. I have a speech therapist three times a week and working with her has helped a great deal. I think in time I can clear it up completely. . . . It almost seems too good to be true."

It was too good to be true. Inexorably, over the following ten years, Bourke-White's abilities to move and act and speak vanished. Bourke-White's illness did, however, help focus wide attention on the plight of Parkinsonism. In June 1959 *Life* ran a feature, with photographs by Alfred Eisenstaedt, on Bourke-White's struggle against the disease. Six months later

"The Margaret Bourke-White Story" (the story of Bourke-White's operation and seeming triumph over Parkinson's), was aired on television.

Before Parkinson's completely disabled her, Bourke-White worked as vigorously as she ever had, reaching out to new areas of the globe, testing new outlooks on dramatic subject matter, and as usual daring to enter realms where no photographer, much less any other woman, had gone before.

In December 1949, several years before she was stricken by Parkinson's, Bourke-White began a five-month *Life* assignment to South Africa. The South African Nationalist Party had been in power there for about two years when Bourke-White arrived. During her extensive tour of South Africa, Bourke-White had ample opportunities to witness the patterns of social behavior the Party's racist policies dictated, and much of what she saw utterly horrified her.

"What are you going to do when you disapprove thoroughly of the state of affairs you are recording?" Bourke-White asks in *Portrait of Myself.*

» What are the ethics of a photographer in a situation like this? You need people's help to get permissions and make arrangements; you are dependent on the good will of those around you. Perhaps they think you share their point of view. However angry you are, you cannot jeopardize your official contacts by denouncing an outrage before you have photographed it.

I like to do my work without lying, if I can. Telling the truth does not necessarily mean revealing the whole truth. I feel you need not give away the pattern in your mind. There is an advantage in having those little mosaics before your mind's eye which will tell the whole story when it is complete—when each piece falls in place. The individual subjects will then add up to something *you* see, not what someone else wants you to see. «

The restraint Bourke-White had to exercise during the South Africa assignment put a tremendous strain on her. As outspoken as she was, and having such strong convictions about racial equality, Bourke-White did not wait very long after departing from South Africa to vent her outrage over the social and economic conditions there. On her flight out of Johannesburg in mid-April 1950, Bourke-White set

After anti-American riot, Tokyo, 1952.

down her impressions while they were still fresh, in two letters to an Indian friend named Ranga:

» I don't know where to begin about South Africa. I'll have to get farther away and sort out my impressions. But it's left me very angry, the complete assumption of white superiority and the total focusing of a whole country around the scheme of keeping cheap black labor cheap, and segregated, and uneducated, and without freedom of movement, and watched and hunted and denied opportunity. And all through such a mist of fulsome phrases, whether it's the vote, whether its a clean house, whether it's a chance to go to school—the patronizing coverall phrase "he's not developed enough for it."

Many things interested me increasingly as I went deeper into them, particularly a really sinister tie-up between the number of people arrested and the question of supplying dirt-cheap labor on the farm. The Government caters to the farm vote. No white farmer works with his hands; he's born to be the "baas." Wages on the farm are so low that even mine work is preferred, although that's bad enough. . . .

As a war correspondent in Korea, 1952.

There is a great deal of illegal brewing of beer in the shantytowns; Africans are not permitted liquor, and may buy beer only from the Government-run beer halls. Even these profits the Government must make itself. So with a situation where any normal development into a better-paid skilled job is closed (I suppose you know that Africans are not allowed to study for skilled professions: even desperately as housing is needed, the Native is not allowed into the carpentering or building trades)—so with this ceiling on opportunity and the desperate hopelessness and poverty of people's lives, it is not surprising that illegal beer brewing is a recognized means of a better income, with calculated, but well-known risks. So well known that the police know exactly where to go. It's a recognized procedure, several times a week, sometimes several times a night, and it's treated like a game.

After much wheedling, I got to go along on one of those raids. Of course, they had been instructed to be better behaved with me. Normally they pull people out of bed, throw off the mattresses, tear up the floorboards. None of that with me there. They just dug up people's yards. But that was enough. It was

this incident that really crystallized all I had been seeing and feeling in South Africa. The sordidness, the atmosphere of terror. I will never forget it. This raid was at six in the morning, people just getting ready to go to work, the police poking into their primitive sanitary facilities, frightened children and women peeping through cracks in the doors, such an invasion of privacy, such a demeaning of human beings, and what an atmosphere for children to grow up in. I will never forget it. . . .

Now about the mines. One thing that's happened to me—not that I ever cared much about them—but from now on I just hate gold and diamonds. Such useless stuff. Brought out of the ground with such painful scraping, and so useless and ridiculous. Especially the gold. Dig it out of the earth in one place, and bury it back again halfway around the world in another. The whole thing makes me really just sick. . . .

The constant supply of cheap laborers, without whom gold couldn't exist—for it would be uneconomic to bother about it otherwise—are kept on the job by the poll tax. The Europeans impose the tax, the "native" has to leave the land and trek to the mine to earn his tax. He has to carry a pass so that his movements will always be under control. Then after working on contract for nine or twelve or eighteen months he returns for six months after each period in the mines. . . .

And such a life. I had been photographing two men and carrying them through various activities. I wanted to follow them underground into one of those mines which go down one to two miles. . . . Then I found that the officials wanted to bring these two boys I had selected to a "more convenient" place. I said that in our magazine we didn't stage anything. I'd either have to photograph them where they actually worked, or give up the whole idea. In the end I won. It turned out that they were working in a so-called "remnant" area, rather unsafe, for the rock all about was honeycombed from ancient workings, also so deep and hot that a miner had died there from heat prostration last November. But they let me go finally.

I'll never forget it. Down 6,300 feet. Which not only meant going one mile down, but in this case was actually 1,000 feet deeper into the mine away from the shaft. . . .

For the first hour I didn't mind it. The chances for pictures were wonderful, once I could get my lenses working, for they mist over terribly from the heat and humidity. But there was that look of real work which you only get from being on the spot—the men had rivulets of sweat pouring down their chests, and their faces just starting with perspiration. But after about one hour I found peculiar things happening to me. I couldn't speak—literally couldn't speak. I had to use the utmost care to make sure I had set the details of the camera and shutter correctly each time—a feeling of slow motion—because I knew if I didn't get the pictures then I'd never in the world get permission to come down again. Fortunately, I had a good assistant who helped me through all my work in South Africa, and without being told he went ahead and set the lights correctly for each picture. And the results are really worth it.

But I only had to do this once, and work for only four hours. But these men come down and work eight hours every day for eighteen months, and actually they're underground a minimum of nine and a half because it takes so long to go those enormous distances in the mine lifts.

And then all this talk about white civilization, and preserving Africa for it, and how well they treat the native in the mines, how well they feed him (they have to, or he couldn't do the work). It's such a treadmill. For when the miner finishes his contract he uses up all his free time getting home again, and before he has time to turn around he must be on his way back to earn more taxes.

Diamonds are a slightly different story. I visited the enormous diamond workings in Southwest Africa. . . . On the diamond workings, the men are slightly better off for they can work in the open sun and air, although they get paid less than in the underground gold-mines. But it's the same system of course, taxes to induce them to come to work, a compound behind barbed wire (with the picturesque addition of savagely trained dogs to ensure that no one escapes with diamonds) and the same unnatural life, herded together throughout the length of their contract.

The whole diamond business is a completely artificial one. The company tried hard to impress on me that it took an enormous corporation to do the vast work of getting the stones out of the ground, but actually everyone in Africa knows this isn't so. On the notorious diamond coast, the stones are so thickly strewn that people could pick them up if they had a chance. But that whole area is forbidden ground, fantastically guarded. Europeans as well as

Africans are X-rayed every time they leave the area; it's a seriously punishable offense to even step off a motor road. In every way, the monopoly on diamonds is protected so as to keep up an artificially maintained world price. . . .

It makes me so angry to take everything out and put nothing back; nothing back into the lives of the men I mean. I think I could stand it better if people were open about it. But the pretense of benevolence is the ugliest thing about it. The "native" is being brought into beneficent contact with white civilization (through being allowed to live behind the white men's barbed wire I suppose). Toward the end of my stay it was hard for me to be even polite to people any more. In the beginning I had to be, for it was a very hard and diplomatic job I had to do, and I did it all—all the officials, the government, all the rest of it. And very hard to get because they know they're greatly criticized by the outside world, especially in America, and especially in the United Nations. They hate the very name of the United Nations. But I got a splendid opportunity to talk to the people I really wanted to talk to.

Needless to say, when you meet the educated African, he is usually an extraordinary person. Part of the constant reiteration of "the African isn't developed enough" for this or that, he "doesn't have the mentality of the white man," he "never will have the white man's brain," is just this fear-ridden knowledge that give him a ghost of a chance, and he'll outstrip many South African white men. I met some wonderful people who are doing a great deal despite formidable odds.

I was often reminded, Ranga, of the opinion you frequently expressed, as to the damage that the well-intentioned ineffective "liberal" can do. Among my South African friends (those who were Europeans), I met many people whose instincts were pretty correct, and yet who deep down fell into the white supremacy habit of mind, and by their seeming liberalism did much more harm than good, I thought—a real peril because by creating a cloak of decency that made things look all right which were really rotten to the core. In South Africa, everything is so bald, so gross that that kind of thing stands out with dreadful clearness. «

In November 1950 Bourke-White was one of the participants in the Museum of Modern Art's "What Is Modern Photography?" symposium, organized by Edward Steichen. The nine other leading photographers invited to sit on the panel were Ben Shahn, Irving Penn, Wright Morris, Charles Sheeler, Homer Page, Aaron Siskind, Gjon Mili, Walker Evans, and Lisette Model. W. Eugene Smith, who was not invited to sit on the panel, was in the audience, and briefly debated with Wright Morris at one point.

The focus of Bourke-White's five-minute presentation for the symposium was South Africa. She began her talk with the following observations: "With the world in the confused state that it is now in, I think that anyone who is in a position to throw light on even a small corner of it is in a position of great importance and great responsibility." She went on to explain that she had never felt that responsibility more keenly than on her most recent assignment, for which she was immersed in a society where "2,000,000 who happen to have white skins manage to keep 8,000,000 people who are unlucky enough to have black skins in a position where they have no vote, where they have very little choice of jobs, where they are not given much chance to get an education, where they are barred from skilled trades. . . ."

The sense of *responsibility* to which Bourke-White refers was a conviction she shared with many other photographers at that time, most notably W. Eugene Smith. The origin of this sense of responsibility is not immediately apparent, however, since it is closely tied to the unique role *Life* magazine played in the United States in the 1950s. Irving Penn characterized *Life*'s immense influence in his presentation for the Museum of Modern Art symposium:

» The modern photographer stands in awe of the fact that an issue of *Life* magazine will be seen by 24,000,000 people. It is obvious to him that never before in the history of mankind has anyone working in a visual medium been able to communicate so widely. He knows that in our time it is the privilege of the photographer to make the most vital visual record of man's existence. The modern photographer . . . , having the urge to communicate widely, is inevitably drawn to the medium which offers him the fullest opportunity for this communication. «

Life magazine made photography America's leading medium of visual communication. The magazine's clout derived precisely from its ability to reach the eyes of millions. When television began pulling eyes away from *Life*, around 1952, the maga-

zine naturally found its power eroding. And with the erosion of *Life*'s dominion, the sense of responsibility to the nation at large, which had made American photojournalism what it was, also faded from the profession. During the era before the many millions of Americans who had faithfully subscribed to *Life* suddenly switched to the tube, the practice of photojournalism in the United States was charged with opportunity and importance, and the most creative of America's photographers responded to the call with brilliant initiative and invention in their camera work.

Bourke-White, for example, pursued her lifelong passion for flying with a spectacular story on the Strategic Air Command in the summer of 1951. The location for the story was SAC headquarters in Kansas, where tests were under way on the highly experimental B-47 bomber. The project was headed by the former copilot of Bourke-White's bombing mission over Tunis, Colonel Paul Tibbetts. Few civilians, even few Air Force officers, had ever been flown in the B-47. Not only was Bourke-White the first woman to fly in a B-47, she was told she was probably the only woman who would ever do so.

» I was to occupy the bombardier's seat for the takeoff. As the copilot strapped me in he asked: "Has anyone told you how to get out of this plane in case anything goes wrong up there?"

No one had. During the next two minutes he briefed me: I must pull a yellow lever over my head—that would blow off my particular portion of roof—draw out a pin under my wrist, give the knob of my chair a three-quarter turn. That would throw up a foot rest, I must hook my feet into stirrups so as "not to catch a leg on the way out," and must keep my head back so the spinal column would be straight and better able to stand the terrific shock it was about to receive. Last, I must set off an explosive charge that would send me and my chair catapulting out into space. I would have two to twelve seconds of "useful consciousness" in which to do this. Out in the sky I would have only two more things still to do: dispose of my chair and pull the delayed parachute knob. Then I could pass out. . . .

Once in the B-47, I was surprised at how little room there was for its crew. Big as the plane is (it can hold more than twenty thousand pounds of bombs and can accommodate the atom bomb) it takes only a crew of three. I worked from two points, first from the copilot's high chair, which gave a quick choice of angles since the seat revolves, and then from the bombardier's nose where I had a good camera rest on the bomb sight rack, since the bomb sight had not yet been installed. Since the cabin was fully pressurized I could work without having my oxygen mask over my face but it had to be connected and ready. There was only one ticklish spot: squeezing through the narrow corridor between the pilot's perch and the bomb sight, which I had to negotiate without being connected to the oxygen supply. At forty-thousand feet, with that meager handful of seconds of "useful consciousness," if the cabin had sprung a leak or if a Plexiglas blister had blown while I was wriggling through the corridor, I would have been out of luck.

Only the great cold operated against me, it seeped through the metal hull of the plane into the heated cabin. Lenses chilled, then clouded over from the warmth of my hands as I used them. Frost crystals formed on the windows until finally there was just one clear pane through which to shoot. Finally that too frosted over and we started down. Only then I realized that squatting on the bomb sight carriage, I had been resting the toe of my shoe on the *metal plane shell.* I could no longer feel my feet. We had swept down from forty to a mere five thousand feet before a painful but welcome tingling showed me I still had toes. «

———

The year 1951 was full of aerial experimentation for Bourke-White. During the late summer and fall of that year she pioneered a technique of photographing the earth while dangling aloft from a helicopter. A striking series of those helicopter pictures appeared in *Life*'s April 14, 1952, issue in an article modestly entitled "A New Way to Look at the U.S." Needless to say, this was a very risky project for Bourke-White, and in fact she had one very dangerous spill. While photographing a practice naval rescue mission in the Chesapeake Bay, her helicopter lost power and crashed into the water. Bourke-White and her pilot were saved from drowning, but her cameras sank to the bottom of the Bay.

In August 1951, around the time Bourke-White began criss-crossing the United States for her helicopter project, her Strategic Air Command photographs appeared in *Life*. Other correspondents besides Bourke-White had, of course, reported on the work of SAC. The early 1950s were the beginning of the Jet Age. The public was developing tremendous interest in the development of America's advanced

Margaret Bourke-White, March 1959. Photograph by Alfred Eisenstaedt.

high-altitude supersonic aircraft, which were widely known to be stepping-stones to our future exploration of outer space.

Nevertheless, Bourke-White's coverage of America's awesome new air machines became the focus of a brief controversy. A report appeared in the press that the Republican Senator from Indiana, William Jenner, had written to Defense Secretary George C. Marshall protesting that allowing Margaret Bourke-White to photograph a "top secret" United States plane amounted to "one of the most serious breaches of military security."

Senator Jenner's protest was by no means an isolated phenomenon. During the summer of 1951, Bourke-White was one of scores of prominent cultural figures in the country who were attacked by the House Committee on Un-American Activities for alleged Communist subversion.

In September 1951 Westbrook Pegler, a writer who made his living by amplifying the House Committee's attacks in a daily newspaper column published nationwide by Hearst, devoted a series of articles to Bourke-White's "Communist" affiliations. The articles by Pegler, which appeared in the *New York Journal-American* on September 4, 9, 18, and 19, prompted Bourke-White to prepare a signed affidavit refuting Pegler's claims. The statement, which Bourke-White's legal counsel, Morris Ernst, submitted to the FBI, is included in her two-hundred-page FBI file.

» I believe in democracy. I believe in it because first of all it enables me to participate in my government and to have a voice in choosing the people who will represent me.

I believe in it because it recognizes the essential worth and dignity of man, and affords equality of opportunity to all, without regard to race, creed or color.

I believe in it because I feel very deeply that every citizen should have a chance to realize himself, to develop his potentialities as an individual, and to make free decisions as to his work and the direction of his life. In my mind, the opportunity for each citizen to develop as an individual is the keystone in the arch of the welfare of the nation as a whole. I am convinced that individual self-fulfillment, with the concomitant result of a healthy and vigorous society, can best be achieved under a democracy. I am equally convinced that dictatorship in any form, whether of the right or the left, means the stunting of individual growth and the creation of a vicious police state.

I believe in democracy because I believe in what it stands for: freedom of thought and speech, freedom of the press, freedom of assembly, freedom of religion, and the right to a fair trial. The importance of the freedom of the press, consistent with the security of our country, is something I feel very deeply. This freedom is my life. Without it I would be nothing. No honest American reporter could settle for anything less.

I am against totalitarianism in any and every form. I have seen it in other countries: in Russia and in Germany. I am opposed to coercion of any kind. I am profoundly against bringing about any changes of our form of government by violent means. I am against any and all political systems in which citizens cannot act and speak out freely, in which they are ruled by fear.

I consider the privileges of democracy to be accompanied by duties. I can remember how much it meant to me when I was first old enough to vote. I

believe one's first loyalty belongs to one's country; and I believe this absolutely and without reservations. I do not understand how any American could feel otherwise. All my life I have tried to make my work help my country, to make it a better and stronger country. I intend to continue to do so.

In view of the foregoing, it is perhaps unnecessary to make the denials that follow. I make them to set the record straight once and for all.

I am not a member of the Communist Party, and never have been. I am not affiliated or associated with the Communist Party, and never have been. I have never knowingly been a member of, sponsored, lectured before, or contributed to a Communist-front organization. I have never been sympathetic to the Communist Party or the Communist ideology. I have never voted or campaigned for or provided funds for a candidate of the Communist Party. I have never advocated force or violence to alter the constitutional form of government in the United States. «

—

Bourke-White went on to address Pegler's accusations point by point. She also appended to the statement a description of her war record, and a copy of the citation she received from the War Department "for outstanding and conspicuous service as an accredited war correspondent serving with our armed forces in an overseas theater of combat." But all of that evidence notwithstanding, the FBI seems to have placed little stock in Bourke-White's defense of herself. Memos about her circulated through FBI offices for the next ten years. Her file was not declassified until 1980.

Bourke-White was mercifully spared the blackballing that amputated the careers of many American writers, actors, artists, and educators who were labeled "subversive" in the 1950s. Far from abandoning Bourke-White, *Life* magazine sent her to Korea in 1952, for one of the most ambitious and challenging assignments of her career.

» I had asked my *Life* editors to send me to Korea for rather different reasons than other correspondents had had. For nearly two years the war had been raging relentlessly with no sign of ending. The various aspects of this confused situation had been reported with courage and skill.

Probably no war in history had been so thoroughly documented. My own magazine had given it brilliant coverage, with David Douglas Duncan and Carl Mydans on the hot front at the 38th parallel almost from the beginning. Howard Sochurek parachuted in with the 187th Airborne. Michael Rougier and another half-dozen of my *Life* colleagues had put their personal stamp on hundreds of dramatic and sensitive photographs. With all the major news services and broadcasting chains, each with its quota of photographers, reporters and broadcasters on the spot, Korea was the most consistently raked-over news center in the world.

Still I felt that there was an important area which no one had covered: the Korean people themselves. Certainly with war sweeping back and forth across their homeland, the people must be deeply affected. I yearned to look into that great undisclosed vacuum that lay south of the 38th parallel. What were the Korean people doing? What were they thinking? «

Bourke-White first made contact with the Korean War in Tokyo. She flew there in May 1952 and photographed the ceremonies for Japanese Independence Day for *Life*. She also shot pictures of Tokyo's violent May Day demonstrations, a melee in which Bourke-White herself became the target of a stone-throwing mob of Japanese students. Many of the rioters, she was told, were children of North Korean immigrants, who had served as slave laborers in Japan's coal mines during World War II.

From Tokyo, Bourke-White proceeded to Pusan, South Korea, where she began a brief assignment on the country's presidential elections. Although she photographed Syngman Rhee and other candidates for office, at that moment the most significant political contest was not being decided at the ballot box but in the rugged mountains where the North Korean guerillas had sequestered themselves.

Bourke-White eagerly accompanied units of the South Korean police on their guerilla patrols, and had many opportunities to question North Korean captives about their activities in the mountains. Nevertheless, she felt frustrated because the climax of the story, as she saw it, seemed beyond reach.

» I was perhaps in a deeper state of anxiety and suspense than usual. I had pictures that I liked and which I felt told a good deal, but I had not found the most important subject of all, which would bind the whole essay together. The keystone should be the human family.... The sub-

ject I was after was a subtle and elusive one. I could not cement my story together with just any family—no matter how photogenic the group might be. I had to find the right family—one that would illustrate visually, and I hoped dramatically, the cleavage in a family torn apart by the war of ideas. «

One day in the town of Sunchang, she found two guerillas who had surrendered the previous night sitting in police headquarters. Bourke-White questioned whether there was any use talking to more guerillas since delving very far into their lives had, until then, proved to be impossible. She overcame her doubts, and began talking to the two tired young soldiers. She immediately recognized that one of them presented the breakthrough she needed: his name was Nim Churl-Jin.

After serving with a group of Communists in the mountains for two years, Nim Churl-Jin had become disillusioned. He had long since been given up for dead by his family; but it was to them Nim Churl-Jin wanted to return. Bourke-White was convinced that this was the human drama she was looking for and quickly obtained permission from the police to bring Nim Churl-Jin back home.

For two days Bourke-White and Nim Churl-Jin drove south until they finally reached the boy's village.

» We got to his front gate. It led into a large courtyard and I saw that his was one of the largest houses in the village. He came from a good family, and he bowed before the gate in Oriental respect. I missed that picture, but I got the rest. Suddenly, he got inside and it was like dragon's teeth sprung out of the ground where all of the villagers and relatives came to welcome him. They were all laughing and crying at once, and he was sobbing his heart out. Then, his wife was there by his side. She said, very simply, "My husband has come home," and handed him a two-year-old baby whom he had never seen.... Then I found that the most important member of the family was not there at all. I had traveled all of this distance to photograph him with his mother and his mother was away. She was visiting relatives in a village five miles away. I said, "Let's go get her." They said, "You can't, because the village is way off the road." "Can't we find her?" They said, "No. She will be taking a shortcut through the forest and she won't be back until after dark." I was desperate and I said, "Let's get in the

Jeep and go somewhere. Maybe we'll have some luck. Maybe something will happen."

And things began to happen! We had gotten only a few hundred yards down the road when we ran into an equally important member of the family. . . . This was the older brother, who was now head of the family, because the father had died. In an Oriental family, the father, or the older brother, rules. Everyone must obey them. . . .

Nim Churl-Jin was jumping out of the Jeep, and I hopped out with my camera (not knowing quite what was going on). The older man began shaking his fist in tears and anger, saying, "You have hurt our country. What crime have you committed that you come back to us again? You went off to the Communists for two years. You have hurt us. We have a good country. What crime have you committed?" Nim Churl-Jin hung his head and said, "I have wiped out my old crime with my surrender." I got the brother to jump in the Jeep with us. I thought he might help us find the mother. We drove and drove. It was more than ten miles. I do not know what it is, but sometimes I think that you spend a whole lifetime taking pictures and you believe that sometime there will be just one which will mean more than any other picture that you have had a chance to take, and you hope that when that time comes everything will be right. You hope that the sun will be shining and that there will be no unwanted faces gazing at the camera, and that those people you are photographing will truly reflect their emotions and that those emotions will be great and valuable ones. Perhaps this was the day, because it was true that the path wound through the forest, but if we had been three minutes later or three minutes earlier we would have missed her.

For a short distance the path looped out across open rice fields and wound back through the woods again. All I know is that suddenly here was Nim Churl-Jin leaping out of the Jeep again and running. I started running after him. He ran through a brook. I ran through the brook too. By that time, he was way ahead of me, because I was having to climb a high muddy slope and I was trying to keep my cameras dry. Way in the distance, down a narrow path coming through the rice field, I saw a woman, in white, running. She was throwing her stick away, and by the time I got to them the two were in each other's arms, and she had her hands on his cheeks and she was saying, "It is only a dream. My son is

dead. He has been dead for two years. It is only a dream." The boy was saying, "No, Mother. This is really true. I am really Nim Churl-Jin." Then they sank to the ground, and she put her arms around him and rocked him to and fro, and I found out that she was singing him a lullaby. Her son had come home. «

——————

By the summer of 1953 Bourke-White had already begun struggling against the impairments of Parkinson's disease. But she still had sufficient possession of her motor abilities to continue photographing for *Life,* and on the usual grand scale. She undertook a long-term assignment on the widespread and widely varied activities of the Jesuits, a project that was, in fact, the brainchild of Michael J. Arlen, who accompanied Bourke-White on the first leg of the assignment, traveled with her to cover Jesuit activities in Honduras, and was then abruptly called back to serve in the United States Army.

Besides appearing in an impressive *Life* essay, on October 11, 1954, Bourke-White's photographs of the Jesuits embellished *A Report on the American Jesuits* by Father John La Farge, published in 1956.

Although after 1957 Bourke-White became too ill to perform a professional job with a camera, her physical impairments did not suppress her drive. When the space race began Bourke-White had herself assigned as the first *Life* photographer to go to the moon, as soon as a seat could be secured on the first available rocketship.

Her flying days were behind her, however. *Portrait of Myself* was Bourke-White's final accomplishment, and her handicap interfered even with her ability to carry that task through. Since she found it almost impossible to use a typewriter effectively after the onset of Parkinson's, much of her writing for the book originated on miniature magnetic dictation discs.

Occasionally, Bourke-White would force herself to type. For one thing, typing was exercise for her fingers, and for another, Bourke-White had always been accustomed to writing with a typewriter. Like Eugene O'Neill, who felt he could only write effectively in longhand, and when Parkinsonism palsied his hands desisted from writing altogether, Bourke-White had thoughts she could express only by banging them out on the typewriter keys. Often Bourke-White selected just a sentence or two from a long sequence of raw material to blend into the larger story she was composing for *Portrait of Myself.* Among those long sequences of notes, there is one in particular, which taken as a whole represents a sort of summation:

» After the war ended, I was thumbing quickly through a pile of books and magazines to catch up on photographs published while I was overseas. I came on one photograph that brought me to a stop. There was only one place it could be. How I wished I'd known at the time. But who did . . .

All at once, the moment of my bombing mission arrived, bringing with it the wide clear skies I needed.

On the day of my mission, January 22, 1943, we were still in the great stone age of bombing. We were loading old-fashioned bombs into old-fashioned bombing planes—our trusty B-17's were monarchs of the skies, although we didn't have enough of them.

As Major Tibbetts helped me up the high ladder into the gaping maw of the elephantine "Little Bill," neither of us could have guessed the strange role of this shy young man. Within less than three years (if one individual could be singled out from the most massive and still most secret group effort in history), his was the hand that plunged this planet into the atomic age. He made the super secret tests in Yucca Flat, and when the fateful day came, it was he who piloted the plane to the segment of sky that overhung Hiroshima, and here he tossed off the fateful Pandora's Box that unleashed the furies which never in the life of our planet could be packed away again.

Certainly Tibbetts cannot be blamed for dropping the bomb. He was just the man at the end of the construction line—a construction line such as the world had never seen, comprising the greatest brains and mass effort ever known to American history. Tibbetts picked the bomb up and at great personal risk dropped it where he was told.

But much more than the atom was split asunder in the construction of Tibbetts's bomb. Much more than the atom was split—our whole system of black-and-white definitions was split to splinters with it. Piercing the veil that hung over the atom did little to pierce the darkness of understanding, has done little yet to establish a goal toward which we can work and hope.

After the war ended I ran into Tibbetts in Kansas.

"Did you realize you were ushering a new era in the history of the universe?" I asked him. He answered "No."

"How did you feel?"

"I was terribly worried until I knew everything was going all right."

"No, I meant, how did you feel about all the people down there?"

"Oh! You don't think about anything like that."

And then he added a cliché (for which we must forgive him):

"They're so poor and miserable it probably helps them as they'd only die anyway."

Tibbetts is a kind and intelligent man, and very capable, I am certain, of accurate observation, if he comes to see things at first hand. To me his unfortunate sentence was a striking example of the remoteness that was troubling me. I was distressed that I could feel no emotion. And, if I did feel, what should I feel? Pity? Perhaps. But what then? Regret? No. It was their lives or our lives, their ideas or our ideas. Compassion, certainly; but something more constructive is needed. Man has been failing long enough in his attempt to solve his problems by battles.

As the battle grows bigger, its purpose in human terms becomes harder to define. The impersonality of modern war has become stupendous, grotesque. Even when in the heart of the battle one's ray of vision lights only a narrow slice of the whole and all the rest is remote, so incredibly remote.

The remoteness between killer and killed in this kind of warfare doubtless has to be there if those of us who deal with war are going to carry on. But what are one's responsibilities? The jigsaw puzzle becomes so complex that no one can be sure which little piece is meant for him and where the edges lie. What should we feel? . . . What can we do?

I can only think in terms of my own field, how a photographer tries to help—how all the best photographers I know have tried to help by building up the pictorial files of history for the world to see. Just one inch in the long mile.

I like to think that our profession can help a little. «

Protester, South Africa, 1950.

Miners signing work contracts, South Africa, 1950.

Men's quarters, South Africa, 1950.

Amalaita fights, South Africa, 1950.

South Africa, 1950.

South Africa, 1950.

Herero women, Windhoek, South-West Africa, 1950.

Gold miners, South Africa, 1950.

University professor, Tokyo, 1952.

May Day riot, Tokyo, 1952.

Head of North Korean soldier, 1952.

Temple mourner, South Korea, 1952.

Captured guerrillas, South Korea, 1952.

Nim Churl-Jin with his mother, South Korea, 1952.

Bridge construction, New York Thruway, 1954.

Levittown, Pennsylvania, 1956.

Strategic Air Command flight, 1951.

Jesuit seminarians, Florissant, Missouri, 1953.

June 14, 1904: Margaret Bourke-White born in New York City.

1906–1921: Grows up in Bound Brook, New Jersey, and graduates from Plainfield High School.

Fall 1921–1922: Attends Columbia University for one semester; takes photography course taught by Clarence H. White; leaves school after death of her father, Joseph White.

Fall 1922–1923: Wins scholarship for year of study at University of Michigan at Ann Arbor.

Spring 1924: Marries Everett Chapman.

Fall 1924–Spring 1925: Moves with Chapman to West Lafayette, Indiana; continues studies at Purdue University. Marriage fails.

Fall 1925–Spring 1926: Separates from Chapman; moves to Cleveland, Ohio; attends Case Western Reserve.

Fall 1926–Summer 1927: Attends Cornell University and graduates with bachelor's degree; decides to pursue photography as a profession.

Fall 1927: Returns to Cleveland to open photography studio.

Winter 1928: Begins her experiments with industrial photography, including Otis Steel Mill series.

Spring 1929: Brought to New York by Henry Luce to work for *Fortune.*

Summer 1930: Travels to Germany and Russia; becomes the first foreign photographer permitted to take pictures of Russian industry.

Fall 1930: Returns from Russia and moves into studio on 61st floor of newly completed Chrysler Building; writes *Eyes on Russia.*

Summer 1931: Returns to Russia to collect material for series of *New York Times* articles.

Summer 1932: Returns again to Russia, and becomes first foreign cinematographer to leave Russia with motion pictures of the country's industrial activity.

Fall 1933–1934: Creates NBC mural in Rockefeller Center depicting the wonders of radio.

Summer 1934: Photographs the Dust Bowl on assignment for *Fortune.*

1935: Begins aviation photography for TWA and Eastern Airlines.

1936: Decides to abandon advertising photography; delivers paper on "An Artist's Experience in the Soviet Union" at First American Artists Congress; meets Erskine Caldwell and begins work on *You Have Seen Their Faces.*

Fall 1936: Signs on as one of first four *Life* magazine staff photographers.

1937: Photographs full-time for *Life.*

Spring 1938: Sails to Czechoslovakia and Hungary with Erskine Caldwell to gather material on conflict in Sudetenland; she and Caldwell write *North of the Danube.*

February 1939: Bourke-White marries Erskine Caldwell.

Fall 1939–1940: Assigned by *Life* to photograph London preparing for war; also travels to Rumania, Turkey, Syria, and Egypt for *Life;* while en route, offered job on Ralph Ingersoll's *PM.*

Spring 1940: Accepts Ingersoll's offer and quits *Life* staff.

Fall 1940: FBI opens dossier on Margaret Bourke-White; Bourke-White and Caldwell travel around United States collecting material that inspires *Say, Is This the U.S.A.?*

Spring 1941: Travels with Caldwell across Pacific, through China, into the Soviet Union; is only U.S. photographer present in Moscow when Germans attack Russia.

Winter–Spring 1942: Lectures widely about experiences in Soviet Union; writes *Shooting the Russian War.*

Late Spring 1942: First woman accredited as a war correspondent to U.S. Air Force; she and Caldwell separate.

Summer 1942: Sent to England to cover arrival of first thirteen U.S. Air Force B-17's, which soon begin bombing raids on Germany.

December 1942: Bourke-White's convoy torpedoed en route to North Africa.

January 1943: First woman to accompany Air Force crew on bombing mission.

Late Summer and Fall 1943: Assigned to Army Supply Services in Italy to cover story of logistics.

Fall 1943–1944: Photographs around Naples and Cassino Valley near war front.

Spring 1944: Writes *"Purple Heart Valley."*

Fall 1944: Returns by convoy to Italy for second war visit.

January through March 1945: Finishes work on the "Forgotten Front" in Italy.

March through October 1945: Travels with Patton's army through Germany.

Winter 1945–1946: Writes *"Dear Fatherland, Rest Quietly"*

Spring through October 1946: First trip to India.

Winter 1946–1947: Tries to write book on India and decides to return to acquire deeper understanding of the country.

September 1947 through January 1948: Second trip to India.

February 1948 through March 1949: Writes *Halfway to Freedom.*

June 9, 1948: Receives Honorary Doctorate of Letters from Rutgers University.

December 1949 through April 1950: Covers South Africa for *Life.*

Spring 1951: Strategic Air Command; experiments with photographing from a helicopter.

June 16, 1951: Receives Honorary Doctorate of Arts from University of Michigan.

May 1952 through January 1953: Covers Japan and Korea for *Life.*

Summer through Winter 1953: Photographs Jesuits for *Life;* feels first symptoms of Parkinson's disease.

1955: Begins writing *Portrait of Myself.*

1957: Last story for *Life:* "Megalopolis."

January 1959: Dr. Irving S. Cooper operates on right cranial area to halt Parkinson's damage.

January 1961: Second operation, on left side of brain, to stem spread of Parkinson's disease.

1969: Official retirement from *Life* magazine staff.

August 27, 1971: Margaret Bourke-White dies in Darien, Connecticut.

Allen, Frederick Lewis. *Only Yesterday, An Informal History of the 1920s.* New York, Harper & Row, 1931.

Arlen, Michael J. "Green Days and Photojournalism and the Old Man in the Room." *Atlantic Monthly,* August 1972, pp. 58–66.

ASMP Picture Annual. Words and Pictures by the World's Greatest Photographers. New York, The Ridge Press, 1957.

Bourke-White, Margaret. *"Dear Fatherland, Rest Quietly."* New York, Simon and Schuster, 1946

    Eyes on Russia. New York, Simon and Schuster, 1931.

    Halfway to Freedom. New York, Simon and Schuster, 1949.

    Portrait of Myself. New York, Simon and Schuster, 1963.

    "Purple Heart Valley." New York, Simon and Schuster, 1944.

    Shooting the Russian War. New York, Simon and Schuster, 1943.

    U.S.S.R. Photographs. New York, Argus Press, 1934.

    New York Times Magazine: "Silk Stockings in the Five-Year Plan," February 14, 1932, pp. 4–5.

        "Making Communists of Soviet Children," March 6, 1932, pp. 4–5.

        "Nothing Bores the Russian Audience," March 13, 1932, pp. 8–9.

        "Where the Worker Can Drop the Boss," March 27, 1932, pp. 8–9.

        "A Day's Work for the Five-Year Plan," May 22, 1932, pp. 8–9.

        "A Day in a Remote Village of Russia," September 11, 1932, p. 7.

    Margaret Bourke-White Collection, Syracuse University

Brown, Theodore M. *Margaret Bourke-White, Photojournalist.* Ithaca, N.Y., Office of University Publications, Cornell University, 1972.

Caldwell, Erskine. *All Out on the Road to Smolensk.* New York, Duell, Sloan and Pearce, 1942.

Caldwell, Erskine, and Bourke-White, Margaret. *North of the Danube.* New York, The Viking Press, 1939.

    Say, Is This the U.S.A.? New York, Duell, Sloan and Pearce, 1941.

    You Have Seen Their Faces. New York, The Viking Press, 1937.

Callahan, Sean (ed.). *The Photographs of Margaret Bourke-White.* Boston, Little Brown and Company. New York Graphic Society, 1972.

Dewey, John. *Art as Experience.* New York, G. P. Putnam's Sons, 1934.

Elson, Robert T. *Time Inc.: The Intimate History of a Publishing Enterprise, 1923–1941.* Edited by Duncan Norton-Taylor. New York, Atheneum, 1968.

Hurley, F. Jack (ed.). *Industry and the Photographic Image.* New York, Dover Publications Inc., 1980.

LaFarge, John, and Bourke-White, Margaret. *A Report on the American Jesuits.* New York, Farrar, Straus and Cudahy, 1956.

Maddow, Ben. *Edward Weston, Seventy Photographs.* Boston, An Aperture Book, New York Graphic Society, 1973, 1978.

Pegler, Westbrook. "Margaret Bourke-White and Her Sponsorships." *Journal-American,* September 4, 1951.

    "More on Background of Margaret Bourke-White." *Journal-American,* September 6, 1951.

    "More on Bourke-White and Photo-Assignments." *Journal-American,* September 9, 1951.

    "Margaret Bourke-White Versus Angela Calomiris." *Journal-American,* September 18, 1951.

    "Girl Spy for F.B.I. Recounts Insult by Picture Editor." *Journal-American,* September 19, 1951.

Shub, Boris, and Quint, Bernard. *Since Stalin, A Photo History of Our Time.* New York, Manila, Swen Publications Co. Inc., 1951.

Maloney, Tom. *U.S. Camera–1960.* New York, Camera Publishing Co., 1959, pp. 228–246.

Siegel, Beatrice. *An Eye on the World: Margaret Bourke-White, Photographer.* New York, Frederick Warne, 1980.

Stott, William. *Documentary Expression and Thirties America.* New York, Oxford University Press, 1973.

"What Is Modern Photography? A Symposium at the Museum of Modern Art, November 20, 1950." *American Photography,* March 1951, pp. 146–53.

page **8**

"I understand that you want . . .": six-page autobiographical essay, Margaret Bourke-White Collection, George Arents Research Library, Syracuse University (cited hereafter as B-W Col.), no date, p. 1.

"the first photographer to see . . .": Portrait of Myself, New York, Simon and Schuster, 1963, jacket flap.

"It is my trade . . .": Portrait of Myself, p. 191.

"in the beginning . . .": notes for Portrait of Myself, B-W Col., no date, unpaged.

"people are much more willing . . .": seventeen-page transcript of Margaret Bourke-White's address at first Choosing a Career Conference, held at Bamberger's & Co., New York, June 28, 1934, B-W Col., p. 8.

"There is something dynamic . . .": notes for Portrait of Myself, B-W Col., no date, unpaged.

"The first few weeks . . .": Choosing a Career Conference transcript, p. 7.

page **9**

"at the very heart of industry . . .": Portrait of Myself, p. 49.

"disastrous to stick to a technique . . ." and *"This is a big wonderful world . . .":* autobiographical essay, pp. 5–6.

"I suppose I have been . . .": NEA feature article entitled "Girl Photographer," no date.

"Art that springs from industry . . .": autobiographical essay, p. 6.

Ben Maddow: *"The closeness of these photographs to the object, their uncompromising focus, their volumetric composition— these are the principles on which Weston was to shape his work from that time forward."* Edward Weston, Boston, New York Graphic Society, 1978, p. 48.

page **10**

"I've had to work out . . .": "Girl Photographer."

"the dignity . . .": Henry Luce presentation to Time, Inc., Board of Directors, February 1929, quoted in Time, Inc., New York, Atheneum, 1968, p. 129.

"Harold Wengler has shown . . .": B-W Col.

"Dizzy Heights . . .": Marjorie Lawrence, "Views of Interest to Women," New York Sun, April 25, 1929, p. 45.

page **11**

"This is to inform you . . .": letter to Bourke-White, B-W Col., June 10, 1929.

pages **11–12**

"I feel as if . . ." through *"the integrated whole . . .":* Portrait of Myself, pp. 64, 65, 70.

pages **12–13**

"I ran into lots of difficulties . . ." and *"I spent a month there . . .":* sixteen-page transcript of lecture, B-W Col., Feb. 1, 1933, pp. 4 and 7.

page **13**

"There is something clean . . .": New York, Putnam's, Capricorn Books, 1958, p. 342.

pages **13–14**

"It is beautiful . . .": thirty-one-page transcript of slide lecture headed "Lecture Russia," B-W Col., no date, p. 6.

page **14**

"There is some peculiar reason . . .": Feb. 1, 1933, lecture, p. 1.

"I know from my own days . . .": conference transcript, p. 1.

page **28**

"A considerable share . . .": B. Shub and B. Quint, Since Stalin, New York, Manila, Swen Publications Co., Inc., 1951, p. 59.

pages **28–29**

"Russia to me . . ." through *"These Bolshevik factory hands . . .":* Eyes on Russia, New York, Simon and Schuster, 1931, pp. 23, 22, 23.

page **29**

"walked into a situation . . .": seven-page transcript of radio interview headed "WJZ 4:30–4:45," B-W Col., no date, p. 5.

"To me politics were colorless . . .": Portrait of Myself, pp. 90–92.

pages **29–34**

"I wanted to make pictures . . ." through *"With such papers . . .":* Eyes on Russia, pp. 23, 24–25, 25–26, 28, 30, 31, 38, 52, 56, 63, 86, 91–92, 92–93, 96, 104.

pages **34–35**

"*There was virtually . . .*": *Portrait of Myself,* p. 92.

page **35**

"*They are so new . . .*": "Lecture Russia," p. 6.

pages **35–36**

"*As we made our way . . .*" through "*I looked through the window . . .*": *Eyes on Russia,* pp. 114–17, 132, 134.

page **53**

"*The work of the women . . .*" through "*I was delighted . . .*": "Lecture Russia," pp. 9, 10, 12, 23.

pages **54–55**

"*I feel that industrial moving pictures . . .*" through "*It was perhaps the most . . .*": six-page typed letter on Norddeutscher Lloyd stationery, headed "Dear Mother Munger," B-W Col., Nov. 9, 1932, pp. 2, 3, 4.

pages **55–56**

"*Tiflis . . .*": one-page note for voice-over narration script, B-W Col., no date.

page **57**

"*The Russian Government . . .*": Feb. 1, 1933, lecture, p. 10.

"*In the hopes that . . .*": letter to Bourke-White from Secretaries [*sic*] Office, 112 East 19th St., New York City, on Rebel Arts stationery, B-W Col., Oct. 27, 1932.

page **70**

Max Schuster's "News Note": attached to note to Bourke-White on Inner Sanctum letterhead, B-W Col.

Oscar Serlin: data contained in Bourke-White Studio file memorandum on meeting with Serlin, June 28, 1933, and letter from Bourke-White to Serlin, June 29, 1933, B-W Col.

"*Miss Bourke-White has decided . . .*": letter from Bourke-White Studio to Lloyd's Film Storage, Jan. 5, 1938, B-W Col.

page **71**

"*I'm doing the rotunda . . .*": B-W Col.

"*At dawn the time would come . . .*": five-page transcript of Bourke-White lecture entitled "Opportunities for Young Women in the Field of Photography," B-W Col., no date, p. 5.

pages **71–72**

Data on NBC mural incident contained in twelve-page file memorandum and three-page letter from Bourke-White to Frank Altschul, Dec. 11, 1933, B-W Col.

page **72**

"*1. To develop the art . . .*": May 12, 1934, B-W Col.

pages **72–73**

"*Three trips to the Soviet Union . . .*": *U.S.S.R. Photographs,* New York, The Argus Press, 1934, unpaged.

page **74**

"*I was doing a lot of it . . .*": "Calendar," twenty-page typed outline, which served as earliest draft of *Portrait of Myself,* contains anecdotes and useful facts from 1927 through 1955, B-W Col.

Eyes on the World: data contained in five-page confidential memorandum from M. Lincoln Schuster, attached to letter to Bourke-White, March 12, 1934, B-W Col.

"*Eyes on the World represents . . .*": five-page typed essay on Bourke-White stationery, July 10, 1935, B-W Col.

"*I had never seen people . . .*": *Portrait of Myself,* p. 110.

page **75**

"*It was one of those . . .*": ten-page transcript of radio interview, headed "WNEW 5:30 Wednesday, May 8, arranged by *Mademoiselle* in collaboration with Henriette Harrison, radio director of the Y.M.C.A.," B-W Col., p. 8.

pages **75–76**

"*Skeleton of a horse . . .*": three-page typed notes for captions, B-W Col.

page **76**

James Wong Howe: letter to Bourke-White, Dec. 28, 1935, B-W Col.

pages **76–77**

"*Mrs. Harrison . . .*": radio interview, May 8, 1935, B-W Col.

page **77**

"*As short a time . . .*": reprinted in Theodore M. Brown, *Margaret Bourke-White, Photojournalist,* Ithaca, N.Y., Cornell University Press, 1972, pp. 121–22.

"Call" to the First American Artists Congress: *First American Artists Congress* catalogue, New York, 1936, p. 5 (courtesy Howard C. Daitz).

"I am very much in sympathy . . .": Bourke-White to Davis, Aug. 16, 1935, in reply to Davis's letter, Aug. 5, 1935; Davis to Bourke-White, Aug. 23, 1935, Bourke-White reply, Jan. 8, 1936, B-W Col.

"The aim of the Congress . . .": model of letter dated Nov. 7, 1935, B-W Col.

"As to the aim of the Congress . . .": B-W Col., no date.

page **78**

"If the Congress of A.A. . . .": B-W Col.

Eastern Airlines job: sixteen-page contract, Oct. 31, 1935, B-W Col.

"unlike any year I have ever lived through . . ." and *"I still remember . . ."*: *Portrait of Myself,* pp. 117, 112.

page **79**

"When the grandeur of industry . . .": "Photographing This World," *The Nation,* Feb. 19, 1936, reprinted in Brown, *Margaret Bourke-White, Photojournalist,* pp. 123–25.

"An Artist's Experience in the Soviet Union": *First American Artists Congress* catalogue, pp. 17–18.

page **80**

"very silent, almost inarticulate . . .": "Calendar," p. 6.

"may not be the South . . .": three-page typed notes, headed "General Notes for Journal-American article," no date, p. 2.

"People don't realize . . .": letter to Dr. A. F. Gilfiland in Corvallis, Oregon, Oct. 15, 1936, B-W Col.

pages **80–81**

"I'd like to photograph . . .": transcript of broadcast on WABC "Gold Medal Flour Show," Aug. 31, 1936, B-W Col.

page **81**

"What the Editors expected . . .": *Life,* Nov. 23, 1936, quoted in *Portrait of Myself,* p. 142.

Crediting individual photographers in *Life*: memorandum from Bourke-White Studio to *Life* offices, March 4, 1937, B-W Col.

"They grabbed that Fort Peck stuff . . .": memorandum to Bourke-White, Nov. 10, 1936, B-W Col.

"I must tell you something . . .": letter to Sr. Oliveira, Pan-air, Brazil, March 5, 1937, B-W Col.

page **102**

Aerosol wetting-agent assignment: *Life,* vol. 6, no. 6, Feb. 27, 1939, pp. 41, 42.

Beaumont Newhall letters: May 10, 1937, and Feb. 6, 1938, B-W Col., reprinted courtesy of Beaumont Newhall.

"picture and word editorial technique . . .": advertisement, *Life,* May 15, 1939, pp. 80–81, quoted in William Stott, *Documentary Expression and Thirties America,* New York, Oxford University Press, 1973, p. 130.

pages **103–104**

"It is not generally realized . . .": transcript of lecture entitled "Lenses Behind the News," B-W Col.

pages **104–105**

Norman Cousins letter to Bourke-White: Aug. 1, 1939; Bourke-White piece attached to her letter to Cousins, Aug. 30, 1939, B-W Col.

page **105**

"Life magazine is sending me . . .": Oct. 9, 1939, B-W Col.

pages **105–106**

"The first was to come here . . .": nine-page handwritten letter to Caldwell, from Ankara Palace Hotel, signed "your devoted wife Kit," Feb. 3, 1940, B-W Col.

page **106**

"The trouble is . . .": letter to Caldwell from Park Oteli Hotel, Istanbul, Feb. 25, 1940, B-W Col.

pages **107–12**

"joint and urgent conviction . . ." through *"Nevertheless, Erskine and I were up . . ."*: *Shooting the Russian War,* New York, Simon and Schuster, 1943, pp. 4, 50–51, 55, 57, 57–58, 195–96, 217, 177–79, 59–60, 59, 235–37, 113, 231, 227–31.

page **113**

"If our democracy is going to continue . . .": transcript of "Town Meeting," Dec. 8, 1941, B-W Col., pp. 7–10.

pages **114–16**

Bombing mission: thirteen pages of typed Bourke-White notes, B-W Col., no date.

pages **116–21**

"I'd like to see the war . . ." through *"In Italy, as on a greater scale . . .": "Purple Heart Valley,"* New York, Simon and Schuster, 1944, pp. 17, 18, 234–35, 62–63, 37, 39, 68, 69–70, 73–80, 109–10.

pages **150–55**

". . . Germany after the whirlwind . . ." through *"We turned our backs . . .": "Dear Fatherland, Rest Quietly,"* New York, Simon and Schuster, 1946, pp. 174, 38–40, 62, 61, 62, 73–80, 174–75.

page **168**

"I had always thought of India . . .": Portrait of Myself, p. 272.

"Consider the great machines . . .": Halfway to Freedom, New York, Simon and Schuster, 1949, p. 83; see also, *Portrait of Myself,* p. 273.

"I do not remember . . .": Halfway to Freedom, p. 84.

"It did not help . . ." and *"Translated into the many situations . . .": Portrait of Myself,* pp. 274, 278.

pages **169–71**

"The decision we have taken . . ." and *"Nanda Lal's little 'East Bengal Cabin' . . .": Halfway to Freedom,* pp. 15, 16–20.

page **171**

'Trying to understand . . .": Portrait of Myself, p. 286.

pages **171–76**

"They flowed in a two-way stream . . ." through *"the weight with which our new and terrible . . .": Halfway to Freedom,* pp. 4–5, 4, 3, 9, 11–12, 25, 22, 27, 35, 35–36, 43–46, 47–48, 231, 231–33.

page **186**

"Parkinsonism is a strange malady . . ." and *"Like all great things . . .": Portrait of Myself,* pp. 364, 369.

"I am glad to report . . .": letter to Dr. McGrath, Feb. 14, 1961, B-W Col.

"I am in simply wonderful shape . . .": letter to Dr. McGrath, March 22, 1961, B-W Col.

page **187**

"What are you going to do . . .": Portrait of Myself, pp. 322–23.

pages **187–89**

"I don't know where to begin . . .": five-page letter "En route from Johannesburg to New York," April 14, 1950; seven-page letter (incomplete) "Between Lisbon and The Azores," April 15, 1950, B-W Col.

pages **189–90**

"What Is Modern Photography?": American Photography, March 1951, pp. 146–53.

page **190**

"The modern photographer . . .": ibid., p. 148.

pages **190–91**

"I was to occupy . . .": Bourke-White draft, adapted in *Life,* vol. 31, no. 9, Aug. 27, 1951, pp. 92, 93, B-W Col.

page **191**

Senator Jenner's protest: "Probe Flight on Bomber by Leftist Photog," David Sentner, Washington correspondent, *New York Journal-American,* Sept. 5, 1951, copy in FBI file #100-3518 on Bourke-White.

page **192**

"I believe in democracy . . .": Statement of Margaret Bourke-White, Jan. 15, 1952, FBI file #100-3518.

pages **192–93**

"I had asked my Life *editors . . ."* and *"I was perhaps . . .": Portrait of Myself,* pp. 329, 349.

pages **193–94**

Nim Churl-Jin: transcript of Bourke-White lecture, "Behind the Lenses," delivered at Town Hall, Curran Theater, San Francisco, Jan. 13, 1953, B-W Col.

page **195**

"After the war ended . . .": typed Bourke-White notes, B-W Col., adapted in *Portrait of Myself,* pp. 226–27.

THE TEXT OF THIS BOOK WAS SET IN PHOTOTYPE BASKERVILLE BY
AMERICAN-STRATFORD GRAPHIC SERVICES, BRATTLEBORO, VERMONT.
THE BOOK HAS BEEN PRINTED IN DUOTONE BY
SANDERS PRINTING CORPORATION, NEW YORK CITY,
ON S. D. WARREN'S LUSTRO OFFSET ENAMEL DULL.
IT WAS BOUND BY A. HOROWITZ & SONS, FAIRFIELD, NEW JERSEY.
THE BOOK WAS EDITED BY OLGA ZAFERATOS AND
WAS DESIGNED BY GAEL TOWEY DILLON.

A NOTE ON THE PRINTS
MANY OF THE PHOTOGRAPHS IN THIS BOOK ARE FROM THE
MARGARET BOURKE-WHITE ARCHIVES IN THE GEORGE ARENTS RESEARCH
LIBRARY FOR SPECIAL COLLECTIONS AT SYRACUSE UNIVERSITY
AND ARE HERE REPRODUCED FOR THE FIRST TIME.
SOME OF THESE ARE VERY EARLY PRINTS, FOR WHICH NO
NEGATIVES EXIST. SIGNS OF AGING NOTWITHSTANDING,
EVERY EFFORT HAS BEEN MADE TO RENDER THESE IMAGES WITH
AS MUCH FIDELITY TO THE ORIGINALS AS POSSIBLE.